Book 1 of *the Tartarus Chronicles*

Elysium

By

Keith A. Robinson

Book 1 of *the Tartarus Chronicles Elysium*
by Keith A. Robinson

Printed in the United States of America

ISBN 9781625099174

Cover art by Jaslynn Tham

www.xulonpress.com

Other Novels by Keith A. Robinson

The Origins Trilogy

Logic's End: A Novel about the Origin of Life in the Universe

Pyramid of the Ancients: A Novel about the Origin of Civilizations

Escaping the Cataclysm: A Novel about the Origin of Geologic Formations

Tartarus Chronicles

Book 1: Elysium

Book 2: Dehali (2014)

Book 3: Bab al-Jihad (2015)

Book 4: Labyrinth (2016)

(dates listed are tentative)

Here's what others are saying about
Keith A. Robinson's *Origins Trilogy*:

"*Logic's End* is a great read, and I highly recommend it. I very much enjoyed reading *Logic's End*. It explores the question of what life would be like on a planet where evolution really did happen. The surprising result helps the reader to see why life on Earth must be the result of special creation. For those interested in science fiction but who are tired of all the evolutionary nonsense, *Logic's End* is a refreshing alternative."

Jason Lisle, PhD,
Astrophysicist, *Institute for Creation Research*

"In this book, Robinson has discovered a "novel" way to communicate vital information to young adults and readers of all ages. Mainstream indoctrination on the origin of species and the age of the earth are regularly encountered, and has long needed combating. Through this unique story, truth is conveyed."

Dr. John D. Morris
President, *Institute for Creation Research*

"*Pyramid of the Ancients* will challenge you to reconsider the conventional wisdom concerning the history of our world."
  Tim Chaffey
  Writer/Speaker, *Answers in Genesis*
  Co-Author of *Old-Earth Creationism on Trial*

"*Escaping the Cataclysm* is an edge-of-your-seat thrill ride back through time. It brilliantly explains the plausibility of the Biblical account of history, especially Noah's Flood. It also explores details of the feasibility of the Ark itself and the Flood's impact on the earth. A great read!"
  Julie Cave
  Author of *The Dinah Harris Mysteries* Series

"Picking up where *Pyramid of the Ancients* leaves off, *Escaping the Cataclysm* hits the ground with both feet running. I found my faith renewed again and again as I was reminded of the many arguments that demonstrate why evolution cannot be the explanation for our origins."
  Joe Westbrook
  Co-author of *The Truth Chronicles*

Table of Contents

Prologue

*T*he first sign of its appearance was the slight movement of air. In the complete stillness of the cavern, even the smallest breeze was noticeable. As the first tendril of wind brushed past the face of the haggard man leaning wearily against the wall of gleaming purple-colored rock, his eyes flew open in excitement.

Leaping to his feet, he scanned the area rapidly, hope sending adrenaline coursing through his veins. Movement to his left immediately captured his attention. His eyes grew wide and his pulse quickened at the sight of the strange purple mist that had begun to swirl fifty feet away, near the far wall of the small cavern.

"It's forming! It's forming!" the man screamed at the top of his lungs, the words echoing off the glowing walls long after his voice had ceased. An expression of panicked excitement quickly replaced the hopeless, vacant look that had almost permanently creased his forty year-old face.

The purple mist began to thicken as it swirled tighter and tighter to form a circular shape. His attention completely enraptured by the ever-expanding circle, the man was oblivious to the sounds of excited voices and trampling feet that were gradually increasing in volume.

The circular anomaly had now grown to reach twenty feet in diameter. Although the edges still retained their gaseous form, the inner disc turned black and seemed to bend, as if being pulled toward the wall of the cavern by some invisible hand. As the man continued to watch, threads of color and light began working their way from the center of the disc outward toward the edges.

The lone spectator of the bizarre event moved closer and closer, his long hair and ragged clothing thrashing in the wind created by the swirling mist. With only half a dozen feet remaining between he and the anomaly, he stopped and crouched slightly, his muscles tensing like a large, predatory cat preparing to pounce on its prey.

Suddenly, three mysterious figures took shape within the center of the disc and grew from mere inches in height to full size within a matter of seconds. A moment later, the human bodies tumbled out of the black disc and fell to the ground at the man's feet. Yet before they had even struck the floor of the cavern, the man let out a cry of victory and leapt over the newcomers toward the anomaly.

As that moment, a crowd of men and women burst through the cavern opening and watched as the man's body came in contact with the swirling disc. Immediately, his body was flung backward through the air to land in a heap several feet away. Despite the painful consequences that the man's actions had produced, the crowd began shouting and running toward the disturbance.

The screaming of the mob roused the three figures lying on the cold stone floor. Dazed, they stared in shock at the wild men and women rushing toward them. Terror gripping their hearts, the three huddled close together with their faces averted.

However, the mob of crazed men and women completely ignored the newcomers. Like the previous man, they threw themselves at the circle of blackness only to meet the same fate. Within moments, the cavern was filled with bodies that had been tossed aside by the swirling mist. Then, as quickly as it had appeared, the mist dissipated and dissolved until not a single trace remained.

Time passed without notice as the occupants of the cavern remained motionless. Then, gradually, a soft weeping could be heard. The sound increased little by little until the whole cavern reverberated with the sounds of sobbing and cries of anguish.

In horrified shock, the three newcomers, a man and two women, continued to hug one another with their eyes closed tightly in a vain effort to shut out the sights and sounds of this nightmare.

"THAT'S ENOUGH!"

The strength contained in those two simple words instantly quelled the tumult. Every eye in the room was drawn toward the speaker. He stood over six feet in height and was strongly built. However, even without his imposing physique, he had an inner strength that demanded respect and exuded authority. Unlike many of the others, his clothes were better kept and were of a higher quality.

"How long are we going to go on like this?" he asked, his voice echoing in the chamber. "Since my wife and I first arrived here four years ago, we've tried everything we could think of to get the portals to take us back. And while I understand that none of you have been here as long as we have, and I know you also want to try everything you can to escape from here, but we need to face the horrible truth:

"For the time being, this is now our home."

At this statement, the sounds of muffled crying began anew. The man continued speaking. As he did so, he walked around the gathering and laid a gentle touch on the heads or shoulders of the others, like a shepherd comforting his flock. "Don't get me wrong, we will continue to search for ways home. We will take the wisest among us and have them study these portals to find a way to reverse them. Others will be given the task of exploring the cave system in hopes of finding a way to reach the surface."

One of the other men rose to his feet and held his hands out imploringly as he spoke, his face filled with raw emotion. "What good will that do, Mathison? From what we've seen, we're not even *on* Earth anymore. This hellish place is filled with strange animals that no one has ever seen before, glowing purple rock, rivers filled with fish that shine. . .we can't. . .we can't *possibly* still be on Earth. So even if we reach the surface, that won't put us any closer to home!"

"You may be right," the man called Mathison replied, "but I believe we should still explore nonetheless. If we *have* been brought here by aliens, as many of us believe, then perhaps we can find them and seek their help to return to Earth. Either way, we have to map out our surroundings to make sure that nothing – animal or alien – will catch us by surprise. Whether we like it or not, we are pioneers facing a new frontier, and we will either pull together, or die."

Mathison paused, letting his words hang in the air and sink into their souls. "But do not despair! Although I, too, long to return home, I would disagree that this place is 'hellish'. It may be unfamiliar to us, but only a blind man would fail to see the beauty of this world! We may be underground, but we have everything we need: water, plants, and numerous raw materials. Together, we can build a new world. Then, when we do finally find a way to reverse the portals, we will have already built an outpost from which others can launch further explorations."

A woman leaning against the wall lifted her head and glared at him, her face wet with tears. "You and your grandiose plans! What good will they do if we all go insane? Or have you forgotten what happened to Kaylee and Michael, the McCrary boys, or any of the other dozen friends we've known who've committed suicide or gone mad from being trapped here? And what about the new diseases we discovered? And how many more young people are we going to lose as they go exploring? This place is no wonderful 'frontier', it is a punishment! It *is* hell! It is Tartarus, a prison!"

"NO!" Mathison snapped, causing several of those nearest him to start in surprise. Realizing what he had just done, he took a deep breath to calm himself. Allowing a gentle smile to soften his features, he tried again. "Julie, I know you still grieve for your children, but don't you see that by focusing on building a new life, we will have *purpose!* We'll have a goal! This will help to *prevent* madness. And the more we learn about this world, the more we can prevent diseases and accidents. But in order to do that, we need the expertise of everyone, including all new arrivals."

As he spoke, he walked over toward the trio that had appeared from the mist. They were still huddled close together, the man's arms wrapped protectively around the two women and their heads down. Crouching down next to them, he laid his hands gently on the shoulders of the man. "Don't be afraid. I know that this is all so frightening and new, but you're among friends. My name is George." Standing up, he looked toward two women who were sitting nearby. "Alyssa, Emily, please take these three to your cave and give them something to eat." After exchanging a brief, apprehensive glance with one another, the two young women did as instructed.

Once the five of them exited the cavern, Mathison continued. "For the sake of those still coming through the portals, we have to pull ourselves together. You all remember when you first came through – the shock of the portal travel, the unfamiliar faces and surroundings, then learning the truth that you cannot return – it can be psychologically damaging, especially if we act like fools every time a portal opens. We need to learn how to soften the blow to those just arriving, to minimize the effects."

Holding out his arms to encompass his people, George Mathison looked toward the glowing ceiling of the cavern. "Come, my friends. Today is a new day! Today, we take our first step toward creating a new future! We will succeed!"

Chapter 1

Exciting News

"Coming!" came the response to the second ring of the doorbell. Eveleen Luschen wiped her hands on her cooking apron as she crossed the last few feet of the foyer toward the front door. "Gunther, they're here!" she called out, her voice filled with barely-contained excitement. Brushing a loose lock of her graying hair out of her eyes, she reached for the handle, turned it and opened the door wide.

"Aunt Eveleen!" the handsome young man on the other side said as he leaned forward and enveloped her with a bear hug, causing the older woman to let out a murmur of surprise. After a few seconds, he released her and lovingly grabbed the arm of the beautiful young woman who stood on the doorstep beside him. "And may I introduce," he said with a dramatic flair, "the soon to be Mrs. Erik Ramsay!"

Eveleen smiled broadly as she stepped forward to embrace the grinning woman, whose face had become nearly the same shade as her auburn hair. "Congratulations, Megan!" After several seconds, Eveleen pulled back and grabbed Megan's left hand. "Let me see the ring!"

As his Aunt bent to get a closer look at the diamond, Erik grimaced. "I know it's not much, but it's all I could afford on my military salary."

Eveleen stood and looked at her nephew. "You've got nothing to apologize for, Erik. It's a beautiful ring. Your uncle and I are so happy for the two of you. In fact, I nearly leaped out of my chair when I heard the news."

Megan laughed. "Speaking of leaping, you look like you're getting around pretty well. How's the arthritis?"

Eveleen rolled her eyes as she turned and gestured for the couple to follow her inside. "It's doing pretty well, for the most part. The new medication is keeping the flare-ups under control – which is a good thing, considering that I'm going to be busy on my feet helping you get ready for the wedding. So, have you set a date yet?" she asked as her guests removed their jackets in the entryway.

"We're shooting for the second Saturday of September," Erik replied as his aunt took the jackets and hung them in the closet. "That way we've got the rest of this spring and all of summer to plan."

Closing the closet door, Eveleen led them into the living room. As they entered, a slightly overweight, gray-haired man with a receding hairline came through the archway on the opposite side of the room. At the sight of his guests, his face lit up. "Hey! How's my favorite nephew and his new bride-to-be?"

"We're doing fantastic," Erik replied, followed quickly by another round of hugs. "I'm so glad you were available tonight. Megan and I really wanted to visit one more time before we head to Virginia to see Megan's parents."

"When do you expect to be back in the area?" Eveleen asked.

"In about another month or so, just before Uncle Gun and I leave on our hiking trip," Erik replied. Even before the words were completely out of his mouth, he saw his uncle's eyes widen in silent warning. But it was too late. The damage had been done.

Eveleen's face darkened as she stared first at her nephew, then at her husband. "You have *got* to be kidding me! I can't believe that you would even *consider* still taking that trip, *especially* now that you're engaged! Did you know about this, Megan?" she asked as she turned to face her nephew's fiancé.

"Yes," she sighed. "That's part of the reason I suggested we come over here tonight. I was hoping maybe *you* could talk some sense into him."

Erik cast a quick glance at her in sudden understanding, then turned his gaze in Gunther's direction. The older man offered no help, however, due to his abrupt fascination with an old family portrait hanging on the wall. Erik gently rested his hands on his aunt's shoulders. "Aunt Evey, you know Uncle Gun and I have been taking these hiking trips into the woods since my parents died. It's a tradition. It's one of the only things I have left that reminds me of the times when *they* took me camping in those woods. Besides, there haven't been any disappearances anywhere within a hundred miles of those woods for over fifteen years. Please don't worry, we'll be careful."

Eveleen's face softened slightly. "I know it's important to you, but. . .but those disappearances are unpredictable. Even the government can't seem to figure out what's causing them. How can you be careful when you don't even know what to watch out for? Besides, you can't just think about yourself anymore. You have to think about Megan."

"I know, I know," Erik said in defeat. Dropping his hands to his sides, he stared back and forth between his adoring aunt and his fiancé. Sinking down onto the plush couch next to him, he leaned his elbows on his knees. "If only you would come with us, you'd understand. . ."

Before anyone could say anything further, the smell of burning food stretched its invisible tendrils into the room. Instantly, Eveleen's eyes widened in alarm. "The potatoes!" Taking off as fast as her arthritis would allow, Eveleen sprinted into the kitchen.

"I'd better go giver her a hand," Megan said to the two men before sprinting off after Eveleen.

Once the two women had exited the room, Gunther sat in the arm chair near Erik and grinned. "Saved by the bell – or should I say, saved by the smell!"

Erik grinned at the bad joke, despite his sour mood. "You know you're in trouble when you have to be saved by burning food because your uncle was just standing there, letting you get double-teamed!"

"Hey, you opened yourself to that one," Gunther replied. "I thought you'd be more tactful then to bring it up on a day like today."

"What do you mean, 'a day like today?'" Erik frowned. "I didn't think our engagement would make that big of a difference."

Gunther shook his head. "I'm not referring specifically to your engagement. Didn't you see the news?"

Erik's frown deepened. "What news? Don't tell me there was another disappearance."

Gunther nodded. "Yep. A whole group this time. Two college kids were out hiking with some other friends. They left camp for an hour, and when they were returning they heard some strange sounds, like gusts of wind, off in the distance by the tents. They ran back down the trail and went to the police, who sent out a search party. They found what was left of the camp, but all five of the other campers were gone without a trace. Your aunt has been pretty disturbed by it all day."

Erik looked at his uncle, his expression dour. "I don't know. Maybe we *should* call off the trip. That's the second disappearance already this year. Tell me Uncle Gun, what do *you* make of all of this?"

Gunther shrugged. "There have been so many strange tales over the past forty years that there's probably *some* truth to them. After all, there've been some pretty well-respected people that have come back with amazing stories of people just vanishing into thin air. Although some of those online videos are obvious hoaxes, it's hard to discount *all* of them, especially the ones showing people getting pulled into those strange rings of purple mist. Those give me the willies."

Erik pondered his uncle's comment for a moment before replying. "I know what you mean. Megan thinks that we're seeing the beginning of some. . .worldwide, massive alien invasion. She thinks that the people who disappear are being taken by the aliens so that they can study us. . .you know. . .conduct scientific experiments on our bodies."

"Well, the universe *is* a big place, so I don't doubt the existence of aliens," Gunther stated casually. "And as a scientist, I *have* seen a lot of incredible things myself. But I still don't buy the theory that these disappearances are the result of alien visitations. For one thing, I don't think that splitting a person's body into billions or trillions of little pieces and transporting those pieces over even *small* distances and reassembling them again in the right order will ever be scientifically possible. If there's any truth to these stories, then I imagine it has something to do with a government conspiracy. Perhaps they created a new, secret weapon that vaporizes people," he said.

Erik seemed unconvinced. "You might be right, but it would have to be an inter-governmental conspiracy, wouldn't it? After all, the reports of the disappearances come from all over the world. It seems a little bit far-fetched to believe that these governments that can't even agree upon the price of rice would be able to keep something like that secret."

Gunther shrugged. "But I also find it odd that it only happens to people in secluded areas, away from big cities." The scientist snorted. "For that matter, it might just be one big environmentalist plot to get people to leave much of Mother Nature 'unspoiled' by scaring them away."

"Right," Erik said with an unconvincing smile. "That wouldn't surprise me. I think I heard that the latest stats said that you were more likely to get struck by lightening than to 'disappear mysteriously.'" In spite of his confident words, he shuddered from the sudden, ominous feeling that settled over him. From the look on his uncle's face, he guessed that he was not alone in his misgivings. *Something* was going on, and until someone figured out what it was, Erik knew that every venture into the woods carried with it an added risk, no matter how small it might turn out to be.

"Well, I think we'd be wise to leave this topic alone for the time being," Gunther suggested. "If either of the ladies bring it up, try to change the subject. Let's give it at least a week, then we'll broach the subject again."

"Sounds like a plan," Erik said. The clinking of plates and silverware grew more frequent, causing the two men to glance toward the kitchen.

"Maybe we should go in there and help the ladies get ready for dinner," Gunther said. "Let me offer you a little marriage advice: helping out in the kitchen is a great way to make points with your wife when she's upset at you."

Erik laughed as he stood. "I'll be sure to remember that. Shall we?"

"After you!"

Taking a deep breath as if preparing to head into battle, Erik let it out dramatically and headed off toward the kitchen, followed closely by his grinning uncle.

Chapter 2

Fateful Decisions

*T*he late morning sunlight reflected majestically off of the water as it cascaded down the side of the cliff, forming a glorious rainbow from the resulting mist that hung in the air. Glistening boulders lay scattered around the large pool of water that collected from the one-hundred-foot waterfall. Enhancing the beauty of the water, wildflowers of various hues grew among the brilliant green grass and the moss-covered trees near the bank.

Gunther and Erik stood near the water's edge, neither one moving as they stared in awe at the peaceful scene. The sound of the waterfall soothed their souls and released the tension from their bodies.

"Gorgeous. Simply gorgeous. Have you ever seen anything so beautiful, Uncle Gun?" Erik asked.

Gunther turned to look at him, a smile spreading across his face. "Yes I have, as a matter of fact. This beauty is nothing compared to what your Aunt Eveleen looked like on our wedding day!"

Erik shifted the weight of his backpack on his shoulders as he grinned. "In case you hadn't noticed, Aunt Eveleen's not here, so you can turn off the smooth talking. Save it for later when we get back. You're wasting it on me."

"Sorry, Erik. As much as I've enjoyed the last couple of days of hiking and camping, I can't wait to get home to see my Evey."

"You're a hopeless romantic, you know that?" Erik replied as he ran his hand through his sandy-blond hair.

Gunther slapped his left hand on his nephew's shoulder. "How else do you think I've been able to stay happily married to the same woman for thirty-five years? With any luck, you'll be saying the same thing about your sweet little Megan decades from now." The smile on his face withered slightly. "It really is too bad your parents aren't alive to see you get married. I know your mother would've bawled like a baby."

Erik gave a wistful chuckle. "She always was a drama queen."

Gunther offered a chuckle of his own. "Just be glad you didn't have to live with her when she was a teenager!"

Erik laughed, then grew more wistful as he looked around at the trees. "Mom used to love these woods. But you know, even though she and Dad used to bring me out here once a year, I don't think I've ever been to this waterfall. It just goes to show that you can spend your whole life visiting these woods and still find something new and exciting every time."

Gunther sighed in agreement as he surveyed the area in silence. A moment later, he pointed toward a small clearing near the cliff wall that was several feet from the edge of the pool of water. "Whattya say we take a break over there and have a snack?"

"Sounds good," Erik replied as he began heading toward the indicated spot. "I wouldn't want to wear you out too soon."

After they had un-shouldered their backpacks, settled onto the ground and began munching on their granola bars, Erik studied their surroundings with greater detail. "I'll have to bring Megan up here sometime. She really needs to see this."

"If you can get her over her fear," his uncle replied. "I was surprised that she even let you come at all."

Erik's sudden silence confirmed what Gunther had suspected. "She didn't, did she?" he asked his nephew after a few moments.

"C'mon, Uncle Gun. You saw how she was last month when we came to dinner at your place," he said defensively. "That was nothing to how she reacted when I *first* told her. She doesn't understand."

Gunther looked at his nephew disapprovingly. "Well, I can tell you something that *you* don't understand: lying to the woman you love is a *terrible* way to begin your lives together. When she finds out about this, it'll likely cause a trust issue that may take you years to overcome. I sure hope this trip is worth the trouble it could cause to your marriage."

"It is," he replied with conviction. "This place refreshes me. I feel so. . .so *alive* when I'm out here. I love the structure of the military, but there's something about being out in nature that makes me feel. . .I don't know, free. I thought that at least *you* would be on my side."

"Hey, I'm just calling it like I see it," Gunther replied. "I agree with you that the women are overreacting and that these woods do something to my soul, but that doesn't mean I want to lie to my wife."

"Okay, 'O Master of Relationships', tell me how you got Aunt Evey to let *you* go?"

Gunther grimaced. "I. . .I played the sympathy card."

"The 'sympathy' card?" Erik echoed in confusion.

"You know. . .I. . .I talked about how these trips are. . .therapeutic," Gunther explained. "How they help you heal from the pain of losing your parents and such."

Erik harrumphed. "Oh, I get it. It's wrong to *lie* to your wife, but it's okay to play off of her emotions and *trick* her into letting you go."

"It's not the same thing," Gunther said defensively. "I didn't *trick* her, I just guided her to the conclusion that I wanted her to reach."

"Yeah, okay," Erik said sarcastically.

"I just want you to have the kind of marriage your aunt and I have," Gunther said more seriously.

Erik didn't reply, and Gunther didn't want to push the subject any further. Letting his gaze wander, he admired the beauty surrounding him. "It sure is amazing here. I think I'm going to sit on that rock over there and soak my feet a little. That spray from the waterfall looks mighty inviting to these tired, old bones. Ya know, I'm no 'spring chicken' anymore."

"There you go again, using your age as an excuse. . ." he said, his voice trailing off as his eyes fixed on something behind the waterfall. "Hey, Uncle Gun, look. There's a fairly large cave behind the waterfall. Want to check it out?"

"Sure. Let's take a look after we rest a minute. After all, I want to be fresh so my old age won't 'slow you down,'" he commented sarcastically.

A few moments later, the two found themselves entering the eight-foot cave. The dampness of the interior cooled their skin and was a welcome reprieve to the hot morning sun. They went in cautiously, their flashlights illuminating the path in front of them, their conversation light, but hushed. However, after only five minutes, they could go no further as the cave had come to an abrupt end, forcing them to turn around and begin the trek back to the daylight.

The return trip was uneventful and pleasant. Eventually, they turned the last corner and stared ahead at the curtain of water that fell down several feet in front of the cave opening.

Erik suddenly slowed his pace and squinted at the diffused light filtering in through the waterfall. "What the. . .? Why does it look so dark outside?"

"It's. . .it's probably nothing. Just a passing cloud or something," Gunther replied, his expression communicating a contrasting message of concern.

With renewed sense of urgency, and the memory of their conversation just minutes earlier still fresh in their minds, the two hikers quickened their pace. Emerging from the cave entrance, they stopped abruptly, their bodies suddenly going cold despite the heat from their recent exertion.

A purplish mist blanketed the entire area near the waterfall and was slowly moving toward the men. The rays of sunlight that managed to make their way through the mist only served to deepen the shadows that fell all around them and enhance the ghostly feel of the surrounding area. The former beauty of the flowers and the water seemed transformed by the light into twisted, horrible reflections of their true natures.

"May heaven help us. . ." Gunther stammered, his knees beginning to shudder beneath him.

Coming to his senses, Erik grabbed his uncle's arm and pulled him forward. "C'mon! We've got to get out of here!" he said weakly, the strength in his voice seemingly poisoned by the strange mist.

The two men ran forward along the path, diving headfirst into the purplish cloud despite their fear. They moved as fast as they could, sometimes tripping because of their own fright and sometimes because of the unevenness of the path.

"It's getting lighter!" Erik stated in hesitant relief, still clutching at his uncle's arm for reassurance. "We're going to make it! Just a little further."

Nodding his agreement, Gunther plodded on, his breath becoming labored. It was then, as he and his nephew neared the edge of the mist, that he began to feel and hear the electricity. The air itself seemed to come alive. The purplish fog began to swirl as crackles of energy became visible. Time itself slowed to a crawl as the speed of the swirling tendrils of air increased. Turning his head slowly to look at his nephew, he could see that Erik was caught in the same time-bending effect.

As if in a warped nightmare, Gunther watched helplessly as Erik tripped and fell to the ground, then suddenly began moving in the opposite direction back toward the center of the mist as if being pulled by his ankles. A panicked scream, distorted by the roar of the wind and the crackling energy, escaped from Erik's lips. Reaching out, Gunther tried frantically to grab his nephew's outstretched hands that clawed desperately at the dirt of the path.

Gunther suddenly gasped for air as the tempo of the swirling air around him continued to increase. Dropping to his knees, he looked back toward the waterfall in shock. What he saw and felt at that moment would be the source of nightmares for years to come. Like water that was swirling into a whirlpool or flowing through an open drain, the mist spiraled around him toward a central opening of light. Instantaneously, Gunther felt himself being pulled toward the eye of the tornado-like whirlwind, even as Erik slid inexorably toward the center and disappeared completely. Although his mind screamed at the prospect of being sucked into that opening, his body refused to obey his frantic commands. Finally, after what seemed like an eternity of waiting upon a horrific precipice, Gunther fell towards the light. . .

Chapter 3

The Welcome Center

". . .beginning to come around."

Although Gunther could hear the muffled words, his addled mind struggled to comprehend their meaning. He felt himself moving smoothly, almost as if he were floating. In fact, due to his muddled senses, he wasn't sure if he *might* be floating.

He opened his eyes, but the images that were transported from his eyes to his brain didn't make any sense. All he could tell was that there was a lot of light. *Am. . .am I. . .dead?* The phrase slowly formed itself in Gunther's thoughts. "Am. . .I in. . .heaven?" he mumbled aloud, just to find out if he could speak at all.

To his surprise, a voice beside him answered softly, as if talking to itself, "In heaven. . .and in hell."

Even more confused, Gunther blinked several times, trying once again to make sense of the shadows that surrounded him. He appeared to be on his back and either floating or rolling on some kind of bed. On each side of the bed were the out of focus, but unmistakable, shapes of people.

Before he could form another coherent question, a gentle hand came to rest upon his shoulder. "Just try to relax. You and your friend are going to be fine."

At the mention of 'his friend', Gunther searched his memory for anything that might help him figure out what was going on. However, his mind still seemed to be sluggish and unresponsive.

Once again, the calming voice spoke. "We've given you a mild sedative to help ease you through the transition. . ." If there was anything more to the voice's comments, they were lost to Gunther.

After an indeterminate amount of time, Gunther opened his eyes again to find that he was no longer moving and his mind was not as cloudy. Based on the myriad beeping machines located nearby and the sterile smell that hung in the air, he realized he was in some kind of hospital or medical center. Outside the single door that led into the room, he could hear the hushed voices of what he assumed was the medical staff. He barely had time to take in his surroundings when a pleasant young nurse opened the door and entered the room.

"Good afternoon," she said with a smile. "How are you feeling?"

Gunther, still groggy and confused, answered the question simply. "I've been better."

"I bet," she replied. "But don't worry, the effects of the transition are temporary. We'll have you back on your feet in no time. Now that you're awake, and since all your tests have come out fine, we're going to take you over to the Welcoming Room, where all of your questions will be answered."

Not knowing what else to say, Gunther remained silent as the nurse helped him out of the hospital bed and into a wheelchair. As she did so, he noticed that he was not dressed in a typical hospital gown, but in simple khaki pants and a plain, light green button up shirt with short sleeves.

The nurse guided his wheelchair out the door and down a non-descript hallway. After passing through several sets of double doors, she brought Gunther through a final set of doors into a beautifully decorated room that had the words,

"Welcome!" written in bold letters across one wall. The room was painted a warm blue with lighter highlights sponged over the walls to create the effect of texture. A six-foot, oval-shaped table filled the center of the small room with plush chairs surrounding it on all sides. The walls were covered with colorful paintings and designs that seemed to instantly put the mind at ease. To the left of the entrance, a comfortably sized projection screen sat against the wall while most of the opposite wall consisted of a large window with the curtains closed. Sculptures and statues were tastefully arranged around the room to add to the overall welcoming atmosphere.

Despite still feeling disoriented and confused, Gunther nevertheless allowed the aesthetics of the room to help him relax. The nurse offered to help him into one of the plush chairs, and he nodded his agreement. Once he was seated, he took a deep breath and sank into the inviting cushion.

Mere moments after the nurse exited the room with the wheelchair, three men dressed in navy blue dress pants and matching polo shirts entered, one holding a thin tablet computer under his arm. The man with the tablet smiled warmly at Gunther as he sat down in the chair directly across from him. The other two men sat near the door, and although their expressions were pleasant enough, something about the way they carried themselves made Gunther feel uneasy.

"Hello. My name is Charles," the smiling man said as he offered his hand to Gunther. Out of ingrained politeness, Gunther shook the man's hand and mumbled a soft "hello" in return. "I know that you have a lot of questions," Charles continued, "and we'll do our best to answer as many of them as we can. But, as a matter of protocol, we need to ask you a few questions first."

Still in a confused stupor, Gunther simply nodded. Taking that as a positive cue, Charles began. "What is your full name?"

"Gunther Wilhelm Lueschen."

"What is your birthdate, including the year?" Charles asked, his fingers working frantically as he took notes on the tablet.

"January 11, 1990."

"What is the current date, including the year?" In response to Gunther's confused expression, Charles smiled again and said, "Just humor me, please?"

Frowning, Gunther answered the question. "August 14th, 2047."

Charles nodded knowingly as he asked his next question. "What is your occupation?"

"I'm a scientist and physicist. My area of expertise is particle physics," Gunther replied, with the tone of one who had repeated this phrase thousands of times.

Charles raised his head at the response, his face lighting up with interest. "Really? That's. . .that's truly wonderful!" Typing furiously on his tablet, he continued with renewed vigor.

The questioning continued for another ten minutes, with Gunther growing increasingly impatient at the mundane nature of the questions. Finally, Charles turned off his tablet and looked directly at Gunther, a smile once more plastered onto his face.

"Thank you again for your patience. We're sorry for the length and details of the questions, but, as you will see soon, they are quite necessary. Now, if you'll turn your attention to the screen, we'll begin the Welcome Vid."

As one of the other men dimmed the lights, Gunther looked intently at Charles. "Welcome Vid? Where am I?"

By way of reply, his host simply pointed toward the screen as it began to play, seemingly of its own volition.

The image of an immaculately dressed man in his mid-fifties filled the screen. He was sitting at a mahogany desk and surrounded by beautiful furnishings not unlike the ones in the room in which Gunther now sat. Casting one last disturbed look at Charles, Gunther sat back in his chair and listened as the man in the video spoke.

"Hello. My name is Devyn Mathison, and I want to take this opportunity to officially welcome you. While I know that you have many questions and are probably very confused right now, let me assure you that every effort has been made to make you as comfortable as possible and to minimize the side effects of your recent trip.

"When you first arrived, we administered a mild tranquilizer to ease your discomfort and you were immediately transported to our Welcome center. Here, you were placed under the professional care of one of our trained medical specialists who made sure you suffered no physical trauma. If you don't remember much of this, don't worry. Through extensive surveys of our past guests, we have determined that this is by far the best way to reduce stress during your transition.

"Now, let me tell you an amazing story that you have the privilege to take part in. Over two hundred years ago, a man by the name of George Mathison, my ancestor, was walking through the woods one day with his wife, Jennifer, when the two of them suddenly found themselves transported, as if by magic, to a wondrous new world full of beauty and splendor. Soon, they discovered that others began arriving, as if chosen by divine selection, to take part in setting up a new colony. As the years passed, this First Colony thrived and grew as additional travelers arrived. The more they explored this new world, the more amazing things they uncovered: new species of animals, new types of plants and minerals, and incredible, breathtaking vistas.

"Decades later, they set up cities and a government. Then, fifty-two years after the establishment of the First Colony, they discovered that others had arrived in different parts of the world and formed cities of their own. Eventually, travel and trade between these new territories increased and everyone prospered. And now, over two hundred years since the First Colony, there are now six known territories: Elysium, the European States, Dehali, New China, Bab al-Jihad, and the United African Nations.

"And now, it is my honor to explain how you fit in. You see, you were chosen to come here by the Forces that control the portals. If you search your memory, you may remember a purplish mist, swirling wind, and electricity. Rest assured, although that event may have frightened you, it was simply the method by which you were transported here. And if you were in the company of others when the portal was opened, you will be relieved to know that they are safe here as well, very possibly watching this same video even now! Once you are finished with the Welcome and Orientation, you will see them again. In addition, the portal also brought you forward into time. Since George Mathison stepped through the portal in 2008, one hundred and ninety seven years have passed. By your reckoning, it is currently the year 2205, so as you explore, you will find some new, exciting technologies awaiting you.

"We believe that you were brought here with a purpose. Each person that arrives has a unique role to play and special skills that can be used to the benefit of everyone. But that conversation will come later. For now, you are our guest. As the governor of this territory, let me be the first to officially welcome you. On behalf of our citizens, we want you to relax and explore the wonders of Elysium!"

A flurry of soaring notes played by a symphonic orchestra accompanied the smiling image of Devyn Mathison as the video faded to black. Once the screen had gone completely dark and the music had ceased, Charles turned to face his guest. "I'm sure you're very excited to begin the tour. But first, I would like to show you what the city looks like from this vantage point. You see, this Welcome Center was built specifically to give you the most amazing view of the city. Please, step over here to the window."

Still in shock from trying to process all that he had heard, and still fighting off the effects of the sedative, Gunther stood numbly and did as he was asked.

"Brace yourself, Mr. Lueschen, for your first glimpse of Elysium!" Charles said with a dramatic flare as he opened the curtain.

Gunther literally gasped in awe. The room in which he stood must have been hundreds of feet off the ground, for he could easily see over the tops of most of the sleek buildings that comprised the city. Majestic towers and skyscrapers formed the heart of the city, backed by what appeared to be a mountain range made of purple rock that shimmered brightly. Surrounding the central buildings were miles upon miles of smaller, but no less beautifully constructed homes, shops and businesses. Vehicles of all shapes and sizes moved along the streets and highways that divided the city. To his right, Gunther could see a wide river of pale blue that seemed to glimmer with its own light. Another wall of rock stood a short distance away from the river's far bank. The entire scene was illuminated by a bright light coming from above that somehow seemed. . .wrong.

"What's the matter with the sun?" Gunther asked as he shielded his eyes from the glare. "The color seems somewhat off." Then, suddenly, his mind caught up with his senses. "Wait a second, that's not the sun at all! It's. . .it's a huge globe!" Turning away from the window, he stared intently at Charles, causing the two other men in the room to rise from their chairs. "This entire city is underground, isn't it? That. . .that *thing* hanging up there is supposed to *simulate* the sun!"

Charles held up his hands, attempting to calm down his guest. "Mr. Lueschen, there are many things about Elysium that will come as a shock to you."

"You've got that right, genius," Gunther replied. Like cold water suddenly thrown in his face, the newly heightened emotions served to throw off the last effects of the sedative and brought back his most recent memories. "Erik! I remember now. Erik and I were hiking, and then. . .we got sucked into the purple mist!"

35

"Please, Mr. Lueschen, why don't you sit down? As Governor Mathison said, your friends or loved ones who came with you are fine. I will personally make sure you get to see Erik soon."

Taking a deep breath to calm himself, Gunther nodded and returned to his chair, his head bowed low. "There's just so much to take in."

Charles placed a hand on Gunther's shoulder, a look of sympathy on his face. "I understand. But don't worry, most people adjust to life here rather quickly."

Gunther's head snapped up. "Adjust? What are you talking about? I don't want to 'adjust'. I want to return home to my wife. I'm not staying here," Gunther stated, his voice rising.

Charles' expression hardened slightly. "I'm sorry, Mr. Lueschen, but I'm afraid that won't be possible."

"What? There's gotta be a way out of here," Gunther said, an edge of panic creeping into his words.

"The truth is, no one even knows exactly where we are," Charles explained. "Yes, we're underground, but, believe it or not, in the past one hundred and ninety-seven years since the arrival of the First Colony, people have been exploring and attempting to tunnel in all directions, hoping to reach the surface, but to no avail."

"But. . .but what about the swirling. . .purple gas. . .or whatever it was that brought me here?" Gunther asked, standing once again to his feet.

Charles shook his head sadly as he stood to face his guest. "Our best scientists have been working for years to find a way to reverse the flow of the wormholes generated by the portals. None have yet succeeded. Mr. Lueschen, this may not be easy for you to accept, but Elysium is now your home."

"No," Gunther said softly in disbelief. "No. I can't stay here. My wife. . .I have to get back home to my wife." As he continued, his voice rose in pitch and volume and he began heading toward the door. "Eveleen. I have to see Eveleen. I told her I'd be back. I can't leave her! I CAN'T LEAVE HER!"

The two men grabbed Gunther by the arms with practiced skill. As they held him, Charles looked intently into his eyes. "Mr. Lueschen, your son needs you!"

Gunther frowned, the words slowly working their way through his frenzied emotions. "My son? But I don't. . ."

"Erik," Charles offered, thankful that his words were having the desired calming effect.

"Erik!" Gunther repeated. "My nephew! He's here?"

"Yes," Charles said. "He has already seen the Welcome Vid, but his reaction forced us to have to use another sedative to calm him. We were hoping that perhaps *you* could talk to him. It would be best for both of you."

Still reeling from the shock of his current situation, Gunther grasped on to this one hope: he was not alone. Erik was here! "Take me to him, please!" Gunther pleaded. Nodding, Charles turned to address his two assistants. "You can let him go. Right this way, Mr. Lueschen. Please follow me."

Charles led the way out the door and down a hallway, Gunther and the two men trailing behind him. After several turns, he stopped at one of the doors, knocked lightly, and pressed a switch on the wall, causing the door to open. Stepping to the side, Charles gestured for Gunther to enter. Eager to see his nephew, Gunther rushed through the door and sprinted over to the bed where Erik lay.

A middle-aged woman regarded Gunther casually as he entered, as if she had been expecting him. "I just gave him something that should cause him to wake up soon." Turning, she looked toward Charles who nodded slightly.

"Thank you, Tracy. I'll take it from here," he said. As the nurse exited the room, Erik began to stir. Less than a minute later, his eyes fluttered open.

Although he was still groggy from the sedatives, his gaze quickly latched onto Gunther's familiar features. "Unc. . .Uncle. . .Gun?"

Gunther smiled, tears filling his eyes. "Erik! Thank God you're okay!" Losing control of his emotions, Gunther nearly collapsed on top of Erik as he embraced him and wept. Despite the fog clouding Erik's brain, his uncle's strange, emotional outburst served to clear his mind and bring back the terrible memory of their ordeal.

Pushing his uncle off of him, Erik tried to sit up, but only managed to make himself dizzy. Gaining his composure, Gunther helped his nephew by propping up the pillows behind his back.

"Uncle Gun, did you. . .do you know where we are? Did they. . .did they tell you?" Erik asked as he glanced at Charles, who still stood in the doorway with the two assistants.

Gunther fought against the emotions that threatened to overwhelm him once again. "Yes. . ." he managed, his voice cracking. Taking a deep breath to steady himself, he tried again. "Yes, they did. I. . .I'm so sorry. We shouldn't have gone camping. I should have. . .I should have listened to. . ." Losing his battle with his grief, Gunther's shoulders began to heave as he sobbed once more.

Grabbing his uncle in another bear hug, the two clung to each other as tears rolled down their faces. Finally, after several minutes of drawing comfort from each other's mere presence, Erik pulled away, his face resolute. "I'm not sure what to believe at this point, but one thing I can tell you: we will not give up! We can find a way back home! These. . .portals. . .they have to. . .I mean, you're a particle physicist! If anyone can figure out how to reverse them, you can."

Although Gunther wanted desperately to believe his nephew's words, his thoughts seemed trapped in a deepening pit of negativity and self-recrimination. He chose to go hiking and camping with Erik, and the unthinkable had occurred. Now, he would likely never see his wife again. *If only I had listened to Evey. . . If only. . .*

Swallowing hard, Gunther's jaw quivered as he faced his nephew. "I'll try, Erik. I promise you. . .I'll do whatever I can to get us home!"

Chapter 4

Tragic Tidings

*G*unther opened the front door of the apartment that he and Erik had been given since arriving in *Elysium* three years ago. As he and his nephew quickly learned, the government had developed a program to provide housing, clothing and other necessities, as well as jobs for all new arrivals for at least one year. After that time, they could chose to stay put and pay the normal rent, or move out. In addition, the government also provided one other crucial service: counseling.

The first few months were critical. As far as Gunther knew, every person who had ever come through the portals experienced a range of mental maladies ranging from depression, to suicidal thoughts, or even insanity. Having faced his own bout with depression, Gunther knew that had it not been for Erik, he would have given up the will to live long ago.

"Erik, are you here?" Gunther called out as he absentmindedly dropped his briefcase and jacket onto the couch. When no reply was forthcoming, Gunther frowned. *His shoes and uniform are still here. It's not like him to leave without them,* he thought. "Erik?" he tried once more as he headed toward the kitchen.

As Gunther stepped into the room, he quickly caught sight of his nephew sitting at the table, his elbows resting on the polished black surface and his hands covering his face. "What's wrong?" Gunther asked, concern sending adrenaline racing through his veins.

Erik looked up at his uncle in surprise. Based on his expression, it was clear he had been so lost in thought that he never heard the other enter the apartment. "What? Oh, hey, Uncle Gun. I didn't realize you were home. I. . .I've just got a lot on my mind right now," Erik said.

"Yeah, I've noticed that you've been pretty distracted lately," Gunther said as he pulled out one of the chairs from under the table and sat down next to his nephew. "Does this have something to do with your recent assignment? I mean, I know that joining the Elysium Security Force was an important step in helping you recover from Transition Depression, but I don't want you to feel like you have to do it out of some sense of obligation. There are other ways you can contribute to this society."

Erik leaned back in his chair, his gaze unfocused. "No, it's not that."

Gunther paused, uncertain how far to press the issue. "Don't forget what Haley said at our last group session. 'It's better to talk openly about things than to bottle your feelings up inside.'"

Erik rolled his eyes. "Yeah, I know. They've been feeding us those same lines since the day we woke up in this nightmare." Although Gunther knew that the words of the counselor were true in principle, he had to agree with his nephew that at times they seemed like hollow platitudes.

When his uncle didn't respond, Erik continued. "Sorry, Uncle Gun. It's just that. . .I miss home. I miss. . .Megan, even after all this time. I just can't move on," he said, his eyes tearing up. "Sometimes the pain and loss are just so unbearable. The only thing that even keeps me going is the fact that I'm involved in the ESF. . .and you, of course," he added.

Standing up, Erik walked over to the window and stared out at the city, the light from the Globe reflecting off of the purplish walls of the cavern far off in the distance. "I understand why so many people lose themselves in computer-generated, virtual worlds, or give in to alcoholism. Some days I think. . .I think I'd rather be anywhere, or do anything than be stuck here." Turning around, he looked at Gunther, his expression filled with such pain and aching loneliness that Gunther had to struggle to keep his own grief from surfacing.

"Erik, I. . .I completely understand," he said, as he stood and stepped closer to his nephew. "But we can't lose hope. Listen, I know it's hard sometimes, but I've gotta tell you that even though I've only been working on the government's Portal Research Project for a couple of months, we've made some major advancements. Up to this point, they didn't have anyone who was trained in particle physics. Since I've come on board, I've been able to show them things that have progressed their research tremendously. I'm very optimistic that we can find a way to reverse the portals!"

"But what good would that do?" Erik replied, his face still reflecting his doubt. "Even if you could stabilize the portals and get us back to Earth, we're still almost two hundred years in the future! Everything we knew – our homes, our families, our. . .our loved ones – their all dead and gone!" As he spoke, the tone of his voice became edgier, his frustration and hopelessness coloring his words.

Gunther looked imploringly at this young man who had become like a son to him. "Yes, we have gone into the future, but that's exactly the point. The portals that brought us here traversed both space and time. If we can just figure out how, we should be able to alter the space-time continuum to take us *backward* in time. And how do we even know *we're* the ones that have traveled into the future? All these people know is that two hundred years have passed since the first people arrived. But how do we know the portals didn't send them *backward?* Time appears to work differently here than it does on earth.

We came through in 2047, only thirty-nine years after George Mathison, but almost *two hundred* years have passed here."

Erik shook his head, unconvinced. Brushing past Gunther, he plopped back down onto the chair near the table. "'*If we can. . .*', 'we *should* be able. . .' – all you have is wishful thinking. Don't get me wrong. I know that if anyone can do it, you can. But even with your knowledge it's still a long shot. We have to face the harsh reality that we're never going back! Maybe we should listen to Haley's advice and *embrace* our life in Elysium instead of obsessing over finding a way home."

Gunther held up a finger and pointed it firmly at Erik, his anger rising. "I don't *ever* want to hear you say that again! I will *never* give up on finding a way to get back to my wife!"

His uncle's intensity served to cause Erik to reconsider what he was saying. "I'm sorry. It's just. . .while *you* have something to strive for, the rest of us. . .just. . .waste away our time."

"Then maybe that's the answer," Gunther said. "You need 'something to strive for'. You need to make a difference. As good as the ESF has been for you, being a police officer just isn't the same as being a Marine on Earth. Maybe you should. . .I don't know, look for something else that will fulfill you – something where you feel like you're making a difference."

Erik was silent as he considered his uncle's words. "Maybe your right," he said at last. "I *do* need a change. I need to feel like I'm accomplishing something important. I can't just sit around doing nothing more than giving speeding tickets and helping *Box* junkies find their way home." Glancing at the official-time display mounted on the wall, Erik shot a weak grin at his uncle as he stood. "Thanks for the encouragement. I'm gonna take a quick shower before I have to report for duty."

As Erik headed off toward the bathroom, Gunther called out one last bit of advice. "Hang in there, son. I'll find a way to get us back to earth, even if I have to die trying. I promise. Things are going to get better. . ."

43

****

The doorbell rang, startling Gunther and waking him from his evening nap. Glancing up at the time display, he frowned. *Who could that be at this hour? Probably just another drunk,* he thought irritably as he climbed out of his favorite chair and walked toward the door. However, his demeanor sobered immediately at the sight of a woman and two men that appeared on the monitor built into the inside of the door. The woman was Haley, his government-appointed Counselor. But the other two wore uniforms.

Gunther's heartbeat quickened. These weren't typical ESF uniforms either – they were the black, purple and silver uniforms of the Elysium Elite Corps. After their conversation that night three months ago, Erik had taken his uncle's advice and submitted his application to join the Elite Corps, the branch of the ESF that focused on protecting Elysium's interests abroad. The recruiters seemed thrilled at Erik's qualifications, and accepted his application almost immediately. Since then, Erik had been gone frequently, traveling to one or more of the other main territories. Sometimes, his unit even ventured into the numerous settlements that were spread out in caverns and tunnels between the main inhabited areas of Tartarus.

Taking in a deep breath, Gunther fought to control the sudden shaking in his hands as he pressed the corner of the touch-sensitive panel on the wall that triggered the release of the locking mechanism. Grabbing the handle of the door, he swung it open.

"Good evening, Gunther," Haley said politely. "We're sorry to bother you so late, but we need to talk to you about an important matter. May we come inside?"

Without conscious thought, Gunther nodded his assent and stepped aside to allow the three of them to enter. Once they were inside, Gunther closed the door and led the small group into the adjoining living room. Gesturing for them to sit on the couch, Gunther sank numbly into his chair, dread weighing heavily upon him. Haley sat on the far side of the couch to Gunther's left, and the two men sat on the far right.

Haley leaned forward as she spoke, her face full of compassion. "Gunther, as you probably already know, these men are from the Elysium Elite Corps. They have something to share with you about Erik."

As she spoke Erik's name, Gunther felt his gut twist in pain. *Oh no, not Erik! Please, not Erik!*

Taking off his hat, the older of the two men cleared his throat and addressed Gunther. "Mr. Lueschen, there was an attack on Erik's unit, which was stationed outside the city of Bab al-Jihad. A contingent of Jihaddist terrorists ambushed them and killed seven of our men. . .including your nephew, Erik."

Gunther felt his whole body begin to shake uncontrollably as the terrible truth sank in. His mind reeling, he became oblivious to his surroundings. Even Haley's gentle touch on his knee went completely unnoticed.

Erik was gone.

Overwhelmed by sorrow, Gunther began to weep. Filled with compassion, Haley crouched next to his chair and placed her arm around his shoulder. She spoke words of comfort, but they fell on deaf ears.

He was now alone, truly alone, with only his hopes to sustain him.

Chapter 5

Brave New World

"*A* booth for two, please," Gunther stated to the hostess of the *Heavenly Helpings* family restaurant. "My friend will be joining me soon."

She motioned for him to follow and made her way over to a booth in the corner. Grabbing a small screen that was attached to a thin, metal arm, she swiveled it out away from the wall and activated it. "Our specials for today are right here on page two. Place your order whenever you're ready," she said in the dull tones of one who had repeated the phrase too many times to count. "You might want to place a hold on it until your friend arrives. Just press here when you're ready to officially order," she finished, as she poured coffee into the cup on the table.

Gunther said a quick "Thank you," then took off his grey suede coat and matching fedora. Setting the items onto the booth bench, he eased himself down next to them, groaning slightly as he did so. His girth had expanded slightly in the past five years since arriving in Elysium, largely due to his penchant for eating when depressed. He knew that had it not been for Erik's help, he probably wouldn't have come out of his first depression at all. But after Erik's death two years ago, there had been no one to help him deal with the loneliness, and his habit of overeating took its toll. Even working together, Haley and his fitness instructor had a difficult time getting him back on track.

He struggled constantly against his growing desire to give up on life, knowing that he was completely alone in this cavernous, underground world. His nephew was gone, and, in all likelihood, he would never see his dear wife ever again. He had no loved ones. . .no family. . .no friends.

The only thing that kept him from giving up was the breakthroughs he and his colleagues were having. By pouring every waking moment into The Portal Research Project, Gunther helped it progress steadily for the first couple of years. He felt a cautious optimism that they would find the answer soon. But then, two months ago, the top Project Manager changed his assignment unexpectedly.

"Man, traffic was worse today than usual."

Startled by the sudden appearance of his friend, Gunther was jolted out of his reverie. "Oh, hey, Travis. I. . .I didn't see you come in."

Travis, a thin, middle-aged man with reddish, curly hair and dressed in a plain, button-up shirt and solid brown tie, sat down opposite Gunther, a look of relief on his face. "What a morning! I had to bribe Janet with a mint-chocolate, layered corkscrew-cake just to let me get away for lunch for an hour."

Grabbing the menu tablet, Travis began scanning it rapidly. "I'm starved. I wonder how the *griblin* chops are. Have you ever tried them here?"

"No. But I've heard they're delicious," Gunther replied.

"I think I'll go ahead and give 'em a shot. I'm feeling rather adventurous today." After he finished placing his order, Travis returned the tablet to it's place against the wall and turned his attention back to his friend. "So, you're looking more glum than usual. Is something new bothering you, or just. . .you know, the normal stuff?"

Gunther frowned as he absentmindedly stirred his coffee with a spoon. "Well, there's *always* the normal stuff. But yes, there *is* something new." Setting the spoon down, he looked up at his friend as he searched for the right words to explain his feelings. "I don't know. You're native born, so you don't understand the desire us 1ˢᵗ Generationists have to return to Earth. This isn't our home."

Travis nodded, having heard this before from his colleague. "Yeah, I can imagine it's hard for you, especially since your wife is there. But as I've told you before, you have to trust the wisdom of the Celestials. They brought you here for a reason, just like everyone else."

Gunther's frown deepened. "You know I don't buy into that 'Celestials' bologna. Why would aliens go through all of the trouble to transport specific humans from Earth in order to save our species? Why would they care? And if they did, then what if they're not benevolent? What if they're keeping us as lab experiments, or for food, or. . .who knows what? If they *are* real, then why don't they communicate with us? There's not one shred of evidence that they even exist."

"Well, suit yourself, but I at least find the idea comforting," Travis replied. "It gives my life meaning when I think that the survival of mankind may depend in part on me."

"Anyway," Gunther replied, steering the conversation back to the main point to avoid any further 'religious' discussions, "I've been really struggling these past couple of months since they took me off of the Portal Research Project." Leaning over the table, he lowered his voice so that only his friend could hear. "It almost feels like the government pulled the rug out from under us just when we were on the verge of a major breakthrough. Have you ever experienced anything like that in your Guardian research?"

Travis shot his friend a disbelieving look, then took a sip of his coffee before answering. "C'mon, Gunther. I've known you for almost three and a half years. In all that time, I've never seen you as one of those 'conspiracy theorist' types. Sure, there have been cuts and changes in the Guardian program over the years, but the rationale we receive from the 'higher ups' always makes sense. They've got the bigger picture in mind. You know as well as I do that as scientists, we often get so wrapped up in our research that we become too narrowly focused."

"If it were only that, I might agree with you," Gunther said. "But, there's something else that bothers me. Now that I'm working on research for the Type I Guardian, I've found myself growing more and more concerned."

"Concerned? About what?"

"Tell me honestly, Travis. Have you ever wondered if what we're doing is right?" Gunther asked, his expression troubled. "I mean, I'm all for human technological enhancements and such, but what about some of the other stuff? I was reading an article the other day about the Trait Selection program for expecting parents. Don't you think there's something wrong with treating children like they are consumer products that we can improve, modify, and evaluate according to some. . .idealistic standard?"

"Gunther, you sound like one of those religious prudes," Travis laughed. "I can tell ya, when Sandy and I had our children, it was fantastic being able to weed out any bad genes and also be able to choose the sex, hair color, eye color, you name it! We were able to get the children we'd always dreamed of. What's wrong with that? You 1st Geners really need to learn to let go of some of your old-fashioned ideas."

Gunther's face reflected his skepticism. "Maybe so, but don't you think some of the new choices are. . .disturbing?"

Travis shrugged. "Why settle for just the basics, when we can *improve* the human species? Why settle for natural selection when we can use *artificial* selection to speed up the evolutionary process? Besides, what's 'wrong' for you may not be 'wrong' for someone else."

"But that's just the point!" Gunther shot back. "What one person thinks of as an improvement might be different from someone else's definition of the word. We may think it's an improvement now, but what's going to happen in fifty or one hundred years? We're the guinea pigs in our own experiments. And if we decide in a few decades that we don't like the results of the experiment, it may be too late to reverse the process. We scientists are often so busy trying to find out if we *can* do something, we fail to ask whether we *should* do it. Don't you think mixing human and animal DNA messes with the very definition of 'human'?"

Travis leaned back as a server arrived with their food, leaving Gunther's question unanswered for the time being. After they had had a few minutes to enjoy their meal, Travis picked up their conversation, his expression more serious. "Listen, Gunther, the stuff we've been able to achieve in the Guardian program has been amazing. We've actually succeeded in giving some of these soldiers the ability to see in the dark, an enhanced sense of smell and hearing, and superhuman strength. And that's just the beginning. However, I'm not going to lie to you, any time you're working with altering the genes of a human, there's going to be some mistakes made. Most of the mistakes are clear pretty quickly in the specimen's life, but sometimes the problems don't show up until it has developed for a few years."

Gunther raised a finger. "Aha. See, you just called this human an 'it'. That's another step in dehumanizing people."

Finishing the last of his *griblin* chops, Travis smirked. "Okay, okay. So I made a little slip. But don't you think the ends justify the means?"

"Frankly, I don't," Gunther replied. "Maybe I *am* just too old fashioned, but I don't think we should be playing God with human lives. Where does it end? Already some enhanced children that have the new wireless implants are becoming more prideful and disrespectful towards their elders because they feel superior. And in many ways they are! They can access data straight from the central network to their brains and do amazing computations that leave us 'naturals' in the dust. What kind of effect is that going to have on society? Doesn't it cause you concern that we're already starting to see the formation of two new classes of people: the enhanced and the naturals? Add those that are genetically altered into the mix and we have a truly frightening social experiment on our hands. If you believe we can 'save' mankind through tinkering with nature, you haven't taken a hard enough look at the kind of barbarism mankind is capable of."

Travis dismissed his friends concerns with a wave of his hand. "You're so pessimistic. That's why we have leaders such as Governor Mathison. He keeps a tight reign on the technology and won't let things get out of hand. Which, again, is why we shouldn't worry too much when we don't understand why the government puts an end to certain projects. They're responsible for paving the way for the future and making sure that every step is well thought out and safe."

Gunther snorted in derision. "You have *way* too much faith in humans. There's an old saying on earth that says, 'Power corrupts; and absolute power corrupts absolutely'. It seems ingrained in our human nature to become corrupted by power. *Especially* politicians. Don't get me wrong. Mathison *seems* like a pretty straightforward guy, but that's part of the problem. He seems *too* good. He's an idealist who's trying to make a utopia. People like that can become the worst kinds of dictators: those that will do all sorts of atrocities because they justify them as being for the 'good of society'."

Emptying his coffee cup, Travis shook his head as he laughed lightly. "Have you been listening to one of those 'preachers' from that Crimson Liberty terrorist group? You make it sound like he's suddenly going to become like. . .like. . .that guy from Earth who killed all of those Jewish people. What was his name?"

"Adolf Hitler," Gunther offered with a snide chuckle.

"Yeah, Hitler."

Gunther wiped the last traces of his lunch off his mouth with a napkin, then dropped it onto the table, his expression becoming suddenly serious. "Honestly, Travis, I don't know how much longer I can do this. These past five years have been the hardest of my life. Every day that goes by takes me further away from my wife. It's getting harder and harder to even remember what she looks like. If I can't find a way back home soon, I. . .I don't think I'm going to be able to continue living. . ." His last words were choked out as his emotions began to overwhelm him.

Startled by the sudden change in his companion's mood, Travis reached a hand out and placed it on Gunther's forearm. "C'mon. Don't talk like that. You're going to be fine."

After a few awkward moments, Gunther had composed himself and successfully fought back his tears.

Thankful that the meltdown had been avoided, Travis decided to change the subject. Leaning back, he crossed his arms in front of him and studied his colleague for a moment. "Gunther, something just hit me. Ya know what you need? You need a break. That's your problem. You've been so driven to find a way back home – which is an admirable goal, I might add – that it has consumed you. It has made you *way* too serious. You need a vacation!"

"What are you talking about? What kind of vacation?" Gunther replied, still fighting the aftereffects of his near emotional collapse.

"*Pandora's Box*, of course," Travis said, as if the answer should have been self-evident.

An expression of unease slowly worked its way onto Gunther's face. "I really don't think that kind of thing is for me. I know it's become really popular in the last ten years, but I. . .something just doesn't seem natural to me. I'm not real keen about having a bunch of techies hooking my brain up to a machine so that I can take a trip to some. . .fantasy world."

"Gunther, you're the most suspicious, backward old coot I've ever met!" Travis stated. "It's absolutely amazing! I've done it several times, and it's exhilarating! You can do or be anything you want. Sure, they're still fine tuning some of the images and modules, but I'm telling you, it feels so real! The technology has come a *loooong* way since it was first introduced. And with the new implants that many people are getting, it makes the experience even easier and more realistic. I think you'll find it quite addicting."

"Yeah. That's one of my concerns," Gunther added. "Don't you think the fact that the government had to step in and *regulate* the machine because so many people *were* getting addicted to it is cause for concern? I read another article a couple of weeks ago about a man that blew his family's entire life's savings to spend more time in *Pandora's Box*. Then, when he couldn't afford to go anymore, he became a drug dealer in order to make more money. Eventually he ruined his entire family!"

"C'mon, you can always find isolated cases about whackos," Travis countered. "But the majority of people just use it as a normal pastime. It's a way to escape from the daily grind for an hour or two."

After giving it a few moments of thought, Gunther acquiesced. "Maybe you're right. I guess I could use a little distraction right now, and I *have* been curious to see what it's like."

"That's the spirit," Travis encouraged as the hostess returned to the table and informed them that their bill was ready to process. After offering their thanks to her, Travis turned back to Gunthar. "You should go to the one over on Clarion Ave. They've got the best setup I've ever seen. If you call before the end of the day, they'll probably be able to squeeze you in sometime late next week, especially if you mention my name. My wife's cousin works there. Ask for Julia."

Looking at his watch, Travis stood, placed his thumb onto the Print Reader located on the side of the booth, and quickly finished paying for their meals. "Hey, I gotta run. Don't worry about the food. This one's on me."

Grabbing his coat and fedora, Gunther stood. "Thanks, Travis - for the meal, and for everything else. You've truly been a good friend."

"Sure thing. Just don't go getting all mushy on me," Travis replied.

"Um. . .as if you haven't done enough for me today, can I ask for one last favor?" Gunther asked hesitantly.

Travis considered jibbing him further, but decided against it after seeing the intense look on his friend's face. "Sure. What's up?"

"Would you. . .Is there a way you could ask around – discretely, of course – to find out about the Portal Research Project? I. . .I really want to know if they are even still working on finding a way to. . ."

"Say no more," Travis said. "I'll see what I can dig up and get back to you."

Gunther seemed immediately relieved and put on his coat and hat. "Thank you. It. . .It means a lot to me."

"Gotta run. See you later," Travis said as he headed for the door. After taking a few steps, he turned back and said, "Oh, and call me after you take your first voyage into *Pandora's Box*. I wanna know what you think."

As his friend departed, Gunther stood motionless for several seconds as he replayed the last part of their conversation in his mind. Finally, he headed for the door as he mumbled to himself, "Gunther Lueschen, what did you just let yourself get talked into?"

Chapter 6

Pandora's Box

"Welcome to *Pandora's Box*, where you can become god. How may I help you?" asked a beaming, young woman with short, professionally styled pink hair as Gunther stepped through the automatic doors.

After pausing a moment to take in the highly polished, beautifully decorated foyer, Gunther cleared his throat and replied. "I have a five o'clock appointment. I was told to ask for Julia."

"Sure thing. I'll get her for you," she said. The woman suddenly stared straight ahead for a second, then she blinked and her focus returned. "She'll be here in a moment. Just have a seat in our waiting room."

Noticing the telltale pinprick of light on her temple that indicated a wireless implantation, Gunther nodded in understanding, removed his grey fedora and sat down in one of the indicated chairs. However, before he had time to even settle in comfortably, a slim young woman in her late 20's came through a side door and approached him.

"Mr. Lueschen, I presume," she said, her hand outstretched.

Rising to his feet, he shook her hand. "Hi. You must be Julia."

She smiled warmly as she brushed a loose strand of black hair streaked with blue highlights out of her face. As she did so, Gunther noted that she also was one of the 'enhanced'. "Come on in. We have a little paperwork to take care of, then we'll get you started on your adventure!"

Smiling hesitantly, Gunther followed as she led him through the door, down a hallway and into a side room that contained a desk and several chairs. Lining the walls of the room were screens that continually displayed images that he assumed were depictions of the various possibilities that awaited him in the virtual world.

"You know, you're lucky you called when you did," she said as they entered the room. Sitting down at the desk, she pointed toward a chair opposite the desk and invited him to sit. "Normally it can take up to two weeks to schedule an appointment, but it just so happens we had a cancellation a few minutes before you called."

"Travis was surprised also," Gunther replied. "I think he said that only a four day wait was a record. Just out of curiosity, how come you had a cancellation? I thought it was nearly unheard of for people to cancel their appointments?"

Julia's face darkened almost imperceptibly. "Unfortunately, one of our clients passed away unexpectedly."

At sixty-one years old, Gunther had become quite adept at reading expressions and could see that there was much more to this story than she was telling. However, he decided not to press the topic further.

"Okay. Well, I know that you're excited to get going, but there are a few things that need to be taken care of first. It'll only take about five minutes if you trust me," Julia said with a wink, "or thirty minutes if you want to read it all for yourself." Taking a tablet from the desk drawer, she slid it in front of Gunther.

"This first page is a standard contract," she explained. "It outlines exactly what you can expect from your *Pandora's Box* experience and gives you some basic payment plan options *when* you choose to sign up to be a regular customer. By placing your print at the bottom, you will get today's session completely free of charge, and you will get twenty percent off of your entire yearly package. And, if you decide to sign up today, we're running a promotion that will take an additional twenty percent off of the price of a *Pandora's Box* implant!"

Recognizing Gunther's hesitation, she changed tactics. "I tell you what, how about we skip all of the talk about the package deal until after you've experienced your first session? I'm sure that once you see how amazing it is, you'll come to understand the value in what we're offering. So," she said, changing the page with a mental command via her wireless implant, "let's just jump right to the liability form."

"Liability?" Gunther said with sudden concern.

Julia gave him a wry smile. "Don't worry, it's merely a formality. This is just a way for New World Corp to cover themselves legally from those weirdoes out there who are always trying to find loopholes so they can sue big companies."

"Have there ever been any cases of people getting hurt using *Pandora's Box?*" Gunther asked. "I thought I read something about people who—"

She interrupted him by holding up her hand. "I know what you're going to say. People are always trying to highlight odd stories or make rumors about companies. Remember, Mr. Lueschen, any time you're dealing with something that raises someone's heart-rate or gets the adrenaline flowing, there's always the possibility that people who aren't in the best physical shape could wind up injured. But I assure you, using *Pandora's Box* is no more dangerous than using exercise equipment."

His reservations still not fully placated, he nevertheless placed his thumb on the reader, giving his consent.

"Great! Now, I'm going to show you a short video that explains how to operate the program once you're hooked into the system." With another mental command, Julia activated the screen on the wall behind her. A moment later, the video began.

"Welcome to *Pandora's Box*, where *you* can become god. This video will guide you through the basics of how to operate the system, as well as describe some of the many options available to you during your session." As the voiceover continued, the images on the screen changed to illustrate the various points presented.

Gunther listened intently, enraptured by the advanced technology, and at the same time, apprehensive about what it would feel like. The sensation reminded him of the first time he had ever ridden a rollercoaster.

After the short video, Julia finished up the remainder of the paperwork, then asked Gunther to speak into a microphone in order to get a sampling of his speech patterns. She explained that this would be loaded into the computer so that the system would respond to his specific voice commands. Once that was finished, she answered a few last minute questions, then escorted Gunther to his private cubicle.

****

Butterflies were performing backflips in his stomach as Gunther waited nervously for his session to begin. He now understood why it took the better part of an hour to get ready. First, they had to get him into the gravity control harness, which had several small, hover plates attached to it at strategic points, allowing the wearer to be fully suspended in mid air. "This is so that your physical movements don't interfere with the artificial sensations created by the machine," Julia had explained. Once that was completed, it took all of forty minutes for the three technicians to hook him up to the machine. Finally, they activated the harness, lifting him several feet off the ground, and did several tests to make sure everything was connected properly.

Gunther stared around the small, plain room in which he hovered. The cold, gray walls gave him the uncomfortable feeling that he was in some sort of cell. It was completely devoid of furniture or decorations. Even the door blended in so well with the wall that it was hard to distinguish. Soft lighting was provided by two rectangular fixtures in the ceiling, and although he couldn't see it, he knew that there was a camera mounted in front of him so that the technicians could monitor him at all times.

"Okay, Mr. Lueschen. Everything is in place. Are you ready?" a male voice said. Gunther couldn't be sure if he heard it audibly, or whether it just appeared in his head. Taking a deep breath, he held it for a moment, then let it out with a sigh. "I'm ready."

"Program beginning. . .now."

The lights in the room dimmed. Suddenly, a screen materialized in front of him and Gunther realized that he was no longer in the harness, but standing on the floor of the room. At least, that's what his senses were telling him. Lifting his feet experimentally, he gaped in awe at the realism of the sensations. Returning his gaze to the screen, he studied his options.

Main Menu
Games
Movies
User Modules
Tartarus Locations
Earth Locations
Historical Events
World Creator

Remembering Julia's suggestion that he try each of them for a short time in order to get a better idea of the scope of what is offered, Gunther reached up with his left hand and touched the word 'Games'.

Immediately, the screen changed and a second menu appeared, listing numerous types of games that were available. After a moment, Gunther selected, 'Mystery'. He worked through a few more menus in order to customize his game, then he pressed the final button that launched the program.

The room around him began to dissolve. Gunther watched in amazement as his surroundings changed. Before he knew it, he found himself standing on a dark street corner at night in what looked to be a small town on Earth sometime in the 1930's. A solitary streetlight shone down upon him.

Despite the incredible changes in his surroundings, Gunther couldn't help but look up. Instead of seeing a rock ceiling, there was nothing but open space and. . .stars! Tears welled up in his eyes as the memories of Earth washed over him. Overwhelmed, he leaned up against a storefront window and regained his composure.

It was then that he caught sight of his reflection in the glass. The face that stared back at him was not his own, but rather that of a strikingly handsome man in his late twenty's who was dressed in a pin-striped business suit, trench coat and fedora. "Well, at least they got the hat right," Gunther muttered aloud.

Reaching out to touch the glass, he was surprised at how real it felt. He moved his hand along it, then felt the brick wall, the door, and even the handle. Despite the realistic feel of the virtual world, it still wasn't quite as natural as Gunther had expected. The more he studied it, the more he realized that things didn't quite match reality. "Man can do some amazing things, but he still can't quite compete with Mother Nature," he said to himself.

Suddenly, from somewhere behind him he heard a woman scream. Turning, he ran down the street toward the sound. He rounded the corner to find an elegantly dressed woman slumped down against a wall. She wore a beautiful red business suit and her head was covered with a white hat with red trim.

"What's wrong, ma'am?" Gunther asked in concern.

When she looked up at him, Gunther felt his pulse quicken. She moved with a fluidity that was *too* smooth – the kind of movement that only a computer could generate. But Gunther barely noticed due to the incredible beauty of the woman. Her full, red lips stood out in stark contrast to her porcelain face. As he stood dumbstruck, she held out one of her white-gloved, delicate hands toward him. Taking hold of it, Gunther pulled her to her feet.

"Thank you, sir," she replied softly. "It was horrible! I was just locking up my shop for the night and heading for home when. . .when it appeared!"

"What appeared?" Gunther asked.

"A figure, cloaked in black," she answered, holding his arm tightly.

Although he was still conscious of the fact that he was inside a virtual world, he was shocked at how the programmers had managed to fool the senses. The woman's hand on his arm felt real, he could hear sounds all around him, and he could even smell the woman's perfume.

An uncomfortable sense of shame washed over him, as his wife's image appeared in his mind. *C'mon, Gunther, you don't have to feel ashamed of being attracted to a woman in a virtual world. It's not like it's real.* Even as the thought crossed his mind, another one followed on its heels. *But isn't being unfaithful to your wife in your mind just as bad as being unfaithful to her physically? In many ways, isn't it worse?*

Forcing the thoughts from his mind, Gunther focused on the story he was now part of. "If you don't mind, sir, would you please walk me to my car?" the woman asked. Agreeing, Gunther listened as she told him more about the mysterious figure while they walked. However, once they reached her car, she suddenly stumbled, then collapsed in his arms. Setting her gently to the ground, Gunther tried to revive her even as the sounds of police sirens could be heard off in the distance and quickly growing louder.

Before he knew it, he was surrounded by police officers – their weapons trained on him. "Don't move!" one of them commanded. "Step away from the woman!"

Raising his hands over his head, Gunther complied as another officer checked the woman's pulse. "She's dead!" he announced, to Gunther's surprise.

Although Gunther was interested in this new twist to the plot of the game, he was also keenly aware that his time in *Pandora's Box* would be over soon enough, and he still had other menu options to explore.

"Return to the main menu," Gunther said loudly. Immediately, the scene around him froze, then dissolved. A moment later, he was back where he started, the menu screen hovering in front of him. This time, he selected the 'movie' option. The screen changed to show several search criteria. Gunther browsed quickly through the available movies until finally, he settled on *The Lion, the Witch, and the Wardrobe* from the *Chronicles of Narnia* film series. To his delight, he actually found that he could select either to enter the movie as an observer, or choose which character he would like to portray in the film. He decided to start with the former and, instead of starting at the beginning of the film, he chose to observe the final battle sequence. After making his selection, the room dimmed as the movie started.

Although this film series had been one of his favorites as a teenager and he had seen it numerous times over the years, he had never experienced it like this. Instead of being limited to the perspective of the camera, Gunther now found himself *in* the battle! Fauns, centaurs, minotaurs and other fantastic creatures fought mere feet away from where he stood in the center of the battlefield. Behind him on the grassy hills were the archers, while in front of him, Peter Pevensie, dressed in full battle armor, dueled with the evil White Witch, Jadis.

A leopard and panther were locked in battle and nearly fell into him, causing Gunther to leap to the side to avoid being hit by them. As he did so, he noticed that unlike the video game, he was wearing his regular clothing. Through trial and error, he quickly realized that although he was inside the movie, he could not *affect* the movie. As the menu had stated, he was merely an observer.

He watched the battle from various vantage points, each time focusing on a different character or action sequence. Several times, he commanded the computer to rewind the scene so that he could watch it from a different perspective. After about ten minutes, he decided to try the second option from submenu. Giving a command to the computer, Gunther waited while the computer froze the action around him, then changed the scene to match Gunther's new request.

As the scenery around him took shape, Gunther smiled broadly. All of the excitement that he had felt as a teen came rushing back to him. When he watched these movies as a youth, he always wanted to be King Peter, and now, thanks to *Pandora's Box*, he *was* King Peter! Looking down at his body, he saw that *he* was now dressed in the full battle armor of Peter Pevensie, including a sword and shield.

The White Witch leapt toward him, her sword blades whirling, but in slow motion. It was then that Gunther remembered the words from the *Pandora's Box* instruction video. "When you take on the role of a character, it becomes more of a video game. You have to act out the part – speak the lines, do the actions of the character, etc. The program will guide you by showing you what lines to say, or what actions to take. Once you get the hang of it, you can even adjust the speed of the movie so that the action sequences come at you a little faster. Just follow along, and have fun!"

As the Witch's blades drew nearer, a red arrow about a foot long suddenly appeared in front of him, pointing down. Following its instructions, Gunther ducked and the swords flew over his head. Another arrow appeared on his sword and showed a thrusting maneuver. Gunther again followed the arrow's lead and thrust his sword at his enemy.

He continued to follow the motions, completing the action sequence. Then, with the initial novelty of the technology having worn off, Gunther decided to have a little fun and see just what his limitations were. Rewinding the scene, he started it over. This time, however, instead of fighting the queen, he turned and tried running away. But no matter how much he ran, his surroundings never changed. Disappointed, he tried another tactic. When the White Witch attacked, he just stood there and let her swords slice at him. Once again, though, he found that his actions just caused the film to freeze. Finally deciding to have one last bit of fun with the machine, he leaned in toward the frozen image of the fierce woman, stuck out his tongue, and blew raspberries at her. Laughing out loud, he took his sword and threw it into the air where it disappeared, only to reappear in the sheath at his side.

This is fantastic! he thought. *I could spend hours in here. . .*

The thought sobered him immediately. *That's exactly what has happened to others. Now I see why people can easily get addicted.* "Return to the Main Menu," he said aloud, his thoughts still wrestling with the implications of his experiences in the virtual world.

Back at the Main Menu, Gunther decided to skip over the User Modules – "Those made up by our other clients," according to the instruction video – and chose "Earth Locations" instead. Tears began to well up in his eyes as he studied the submenu. Most of the major cities across the globe, such as Paris, London, New York, Hong Kong, and Jerusalem were listed, as well as major sites like the Grand Canyon, The Great Wall of China, and Niagara Falls. In a daze, Gunther accessed the program for Paris, and made a specific selection on the map of the city. In a moment, the menu disappeared and Gunther found himself staring up at a digital rendition of the Eiffel Tower.

As he stood in the plaza, the virtual world seemed to fade as Gunther found himself caught up in his own memories. He remembered walking beneath the Tower, holding hands with Eveleen as they took in the sights. Although he knew he could spend hours visiting the different locations available in the program, he also knew that each location would only serve to increase his longing to return to Earth. "Return to the Main Menu."

Having become familiar with the workings of the program, Gunther spent only a moment selecting the "Historical Events" feature from the Main Menu. After reading through the list of possible choices, he paused, trying to decide which to visit. With his thoughts still thinking of his wife, he decided to pick an event that she would have been interested in: "The Crucifixion of Jesus."

The scenery around him changed to show the ancient city of Jerusalem. Again, Gunther found that the computer imagery, as amazing as it was, still had a fake quality to it. He was standing in a courtyard that was filled with an angry crowd. And, similar to the movie program, he quickly discovered that he was only a spectator, not a participant in the program.

Pontius Pilate, the Roman prefect, looked down upon the crowd, a bruised and battered man wearing a purple robe and white loincloth standing next to him. Pontius Pilate quieted the crowd as Gunther climbed the steps toward the men in order to get a better view. The Jesus that stood before him looked like someone from a Hollywood movie. He was handsome, and although he was bruised and beaten, the blood that ran down his computer generated abdomen looked thin and unrealistic.

"Are you the Son of God?" Pilate asked Jesus in a loud voice so that the crowd could hear. Jesus shook his head and looked directly at the people. "I am *a* Son of God. The Kingdom of Heaven is within each of us."

Gunther frowned at the words. As an atheist, he wouldn't have called himself versed in the Bible, but Eveleen knew it quite well. In fact, he remembered an argument they had had about this very topic. He didn't know what Jesus had replied, but he was sure this wasn't it. The makers of *Pandora's Box* had obviously not done their homework. *Unless. . .they did this deliberately,* he thought uneasily.

Suddenly, an idea struck him that caused his stomach to turn. He remembered the articles he had read about how the government was investing money to buy scaled down versions of *Pandora's Box* for the public school system. *This virtual world, this machine, is being used to educate. With it, the programmers can change history, and because it is presented in such a powerful way, the masses will believe it unquestioningly. They are rewriting history to suit their own agendas. What other changes have they made to history?*

I guess like every other tool, it's a matter of who is using it. If used properly, this machine could be an incredible teaching tool. But, if misused, it could become a device used for brainwashing, and if combined with the other entertainment features, a tool to promote all kinds of social evils and perverse behaviors.

Still mulling over his disturbing thoughts, Gunther returned to the Main Menu and chose the final selection, "World Creator." He worked through several more menus in order to set the parameters of his new world. When he was finished, the program began. Within moments, he found himself standing in a wide-open field on Earth that stretched to the horizon in every direction. Following the instructions he was given in the video prior to his session, he said, "Create mountains." Immediately, a screen appeared before him showing several types of mountain ranges. "Selection E, placement fifty miles from center, size 70%." A moment later, snow-capped mountains appeared to his right. "Reduce height to 80%," Gunther said. The height of the mountains shrunk slightly.

Awed by the sheer possibilities of what he could accomplish with this program, he continued with renewed vigor. "Create river." Again, the screen appeared showing various river choices. "Selection J, placement fifteen miles from center, length twenty miles north and ten miles south from center."

Gunther quickly became so immersed in the creation of his world, that he lost track of time. He was therefore shocked when his handiwork began to dissolve and the plain, nondescript room came back into focus. After two hours in the virtual world, it took Gunther a second to remember where he was and why he was in a harness and hanging several feet off of the floor.

Before long, the technicians had him unhooked and back on his feet. Julia met him as he exited from the room, his mind still reeling from all that he had experienced. "Well, what did you think? Didn't I tell you it was amazing?"

"Yes," Gunther responded dumbly, "one could get lost in there."

Although he didn't intend it as a compliment, she took the comment and ran with it. "I know, right? One time, I *did* get lost in my own created world. But rather than just jump back to the main menu, I explored for awhile and made a game out of finding my way back to the mansion I created. And time seems to pass so quickly, doesn't it?"

"Yeah," was all Gunther could manage to say.

"So, why don't you come in here to my office and let's talk about our packages?"

An hour later, Gunther left *Pandora's Box* with a two year session agreement and an appointment to receive the *Pandora's Box* implant. Despite his misgivings and uncertainty, his desire to return to the virtual world overrode his concerns. He soon found himself at home, even though his return drive was a blur due to the excitement of his recent experience and his tumultuous thoughts about the uses of the technology. Entering his apartment, he finally remembered that he had not eaten all afternoon. He headed into his kitchen to search for something to eat.

Suddenly, he felt a body press up against him as a hand covered his mouth. Gunther stiffened and tried to cry out, but Travis's voice whispered quickly in his ear. "Gunther, it's me. I'm going to let you go, but I need you to keep quiet."

As soon as the hand was removed from his mouth, Gunther spun around to face his friend. "What are you doing?" he said in a harsh whisper. "You scared me half to death!"

Travis merely stared back at him, his face ashen. "I don't have much time. I. . .I'm leaving Elysium tonight."

Stunned by the cryptic tone of his voice, Gunther became immediately serious. "Why? What. . .what's going on?"

"You were right, Gunther. The government did pull the plug on your project for a reason."

Gunther felt his skin go cold. "Why?"

"They never were interested in stabilizing the portals," Travis continued. "They were. . .they were making a weapon!"

Chapter 7

Government Coverup

"What?" was all Gunther could manage to push past lips that had suddenly gone dry.

"Yes!" Travis said. "An incredible weapon."

Gunther stood unmoving for several seconds, as if turned to stone. Finally, his thoughts sorted themselves out enough to form a coherent sentence. When they did, the questions came tumbling out in rapid succession. "But. . .how could they. . .how could my research be used to create a weapon? And why? We're not at war. And why are you leaving? What about your family? Where will you go?"

Travis placed a weary hand against his head as he sunk into a chair in the attached dining room. "Honestly, I'm already in over my head here, so I can't give you all the details. I *can* tell you what I found. I don't have much time, but I'll at least give you the short version. Why don't you sit down?"

Moving as if in slow motion, Gunther sat down at the dining room table in the chair across from Travis. Once he was seated, his friend began. "When you asked me on Tuesday to check into the Portal Research Project, I started by contacting a colleague of mine who is a supervisor over several projects. He owed me a favor, so he gladly did some digging. He came back a day later and gave me the official document that showed that the project had been closed. However, as I read it over, I could tell that something didn't seem right, but I couldn't put my finger on it.

"It wasn't until two days later that I realized what was wrong. The date of the termination of the project didn't match what you had told me, and the location of the stored materials used in the project couldn't have been correct."

"Why was that?" Gunther asked.

"Because I have access to the room where the materials were supposed to be located, and I can tell you for a fact that they're not there," Travis replied.

"So then, where are they?" his friend asked worriedly.

"That's what I wanted to know, so I did some more digging," Travis added. "I have another friend who works in security at the Research and Records compound. When I told him what was going on, he became intrigued. He couldn't do the research himself, but he changed my access privileges so that I could go into the archives. That's where I found out about the weapon."

"Did you find out what the weapon was supposed to do?" Gunther asked.

Travis shook his head. "Not really, but I did find a top-secret memo that stated that the Portal Research Project had had a breakthrough that could have military significance. Here," he said as he handed Gunther a mini storage drive. "This has all of the info I could find."

"I still don't understand," Gunther stated. "Why would they make a weapon?"

"Haven't you learned any of the history of Tartarus since you arrived?"

Gunther furrowed his brow. "Yes, some. Why?"

"After the six territories of Tartarus finally connected, they formed treaties and agreements so that trade and travel could flourish. This continued for many years until the leaders of

Bab al-Jihad decided that they would wage jihad on the other cities. Ever heard of the War of 163?"

"Yes, I have," Gunther said. "But that was almost forty years ago. Are you telling me that the government of Elysium is afraid of another attack?"

Travis nodded. "Yep. They're using your portal research to make a secret weapon, and that's why they started development of the Guardian program. The Guardians aren't just to 'keep the peace,' as their propaganda states. Their real purpose, according to the documents I found, is to be prepared to strike at the Jihadists! Governor Mathison is preparing for another war!"

"So, that's why you're leaving the city," Gunther stated, matter-of-factly.

"There's more to it than that," Travis said as he looked around hastily, as if expecting a Guardian to jump out of the woodwork at any second. "I'm leaving because. . .I made a mistake. My friend told me to make sure I deleted any trace that I had used the archives. But the discovery of the weapon and the impending war rattled me so much, I failed to erase the history. So. . .it's just a matter of time until they know I was there. If they went through so much trouble to hide the project's existence, then they're sure to come after me.

"I've got to admit, Gunther, you were right," Travis continued. "The government has been hiding things from us, and that scares me to death. I'm not going to wait around until they take me, or until my family gets killed in a war. I'm getting out now."

"Don't you think you're overreacting a little?" Gunther asked. "I don't trust the government, but I don't think they'd actually hurt your family. Wouldn't you think we'd have a little more warning before the war starts?"

Travis shrugged. "I wouldn't put anything past them at this point. You need to read the files I gave you. There's some stuff in there that will rob you of sleep."

"But where will you go?" Gunther asked in concern.

"I don't know. Hopefully my family and I can start over somewhere. We're heading for Dehali," Travis said. "I'm even considering some of the outlands or undeveloped territory. At least then we might be able to escape the war. Gunther, if a war starts between Bab al-Jihad and Elysium, all of Tartarus could be pulled in. I came here tonight to invite you to come with us."

Gunther sat in silence, trying to make sense of everything he'd been told. Despite his concern about the war, his mind kept coming back to one thing: the Portal Research Project. The government hadn't just shut it down, they had taken the research and turned it into a weapon of some kind. *Which means, they didn't even* try *using our research to stabilize the portals! The original project may still work! If I could get my hands on the Portal Stabilizer, I might be able to finish it and open up a way back to earth!*

The thought sent a shiver of excitement down his spine. Leaning in toward Travis, Gunther shot him a look of such intensity that his friend moved backward slightly in surprise. "What was the name of your friend who works in security?"

Travis paused before replying. "Juan. Why?"

"Do you think he could change my access also?"

"Why? What are you thinking?" Travis said, not liking the look on his friend's face.

Standing up, Gunther began to pace back and forth as a plan started to form in his mind. "If they still have our prototype for the Portal Stabilizer, and if I could get my hands on it, I might be able to complete the original project! I'd need to be able to get into the facility, of course. They might not even know the prototype was missing if they aren't using it anymore, and I could just make a copy of the original data. Then, once we have it, we could take it to another city and finish the research there. I might be able to get us back to earth!"

"I don't know, Gunther," Travis said uncertainly. "Why take the risk? Can't you just come with us and start over? You worked on the project in Elysium. Why not just build another prototype somewhere far from here?"

Gunther frowned. "It's not that easy. I worked with a whole team of scientists, and we built upon the work of others. Without those notes, I don't think I could do it on my own."

Travis stared hard at his best friend for nearly a minute without saying a word. Finally, he walked up to him and placed a hand on his shoulder, causing Gunther to stop pacing. "You've been a great friend, and I don't want to see you get hurt. If you try to get into that facility, you'll likely get caught."

Returning his friend's stare, Gunther's face softened. "Thanks for your concern, but as I've told you before, the only thing that matters to me is getting back to earth to see Eveleen. This is the best chance I have to make that a reality. And if I get caught trying, then at least I'll spend the rest of my days in this God-forsaken underworld knowing that I did everything I could to get home. I have to try."

The expression on Travis' face made it clear that he disapproved of Gunther's course of action. "Yes, but will you be able to endure the torture?" he said, trying to dissuade his friend. "Would Eveleen want you to suffer like that? Besides, you'd never get in and out of there without help."

"What about your friend, Juan?" Gunther asked, his face brightening. "Would he be willing to help me?"

Travis frowned. "I don't think so. He stuck his neck out for me once, but that was a small matter compared to what you're asking him to do."

"Please!" Gunther pleaded. "Just ask him. If he says 'no', then perhaps I'll reconsider the whole plan."

After a moment of consideration, Travis conceded. "Fine. I'll ask him, but don't get your hopes up. And if he says 'no', then I urge you to forget the whole thing. If, by some miracle, he *does* say 'yes', then I'll have him contact you directly. Either way, regardless of what happens, if you're still able, try to make it to Dehali. I'll leave a message for you at the Om Tower Hotel near the center of the city letting you know how to get in contact with me."

"Thank you, Travis. Thank you for everything."

"No problem," he replied. "You know I wouldn't do this for anyone else. Don't make me regret doing this for you. Good luck, my friend.

With nothing more to say, Travis embraced his friend, then left the apartment. As soon as he was gone, Gunther took the mini storage drive, popped it into his computer and began to read. He knew that, one way or another, his life was about to change drastically and he wanted to do everything in his power to be prepared for what lie ahead.

Chapter 8

Infiltration

Gunther's pulse quickened as he climbed the steps toward the entrance of the massive, government building. The Globe, the large, yellowish-orange ball of light that simulated the sun and moon, was nearly to the end of the mechanized track that moved it across the ceiling of the enormous cavern that housed the city of Elysium. In just a few more hours, its light would dim and change into the pale blue representing the moon and would reverse direction along the track. When that happened, Gunther needed to already be in place, or his plan would fail.

When he had received the call from Juan, he'd been both excited and terrified. Amazingly, Travis' friend had agreed to help, and now Gunther found himself standing at the front entrance, about to attempt to break into a secured area of the government building. Taking a deep breath to calm himself, he stepped through the wide, double doors.

His normal, research scientist clearance allowed him to easily enter the building without any problems. From there, Gunther took the elevator up to the ninth floor of the building and waited in one of the many employee lounges. Time seemed to stand still as he waited. . .and waited. Finally, as the chronometer reached 8:12 PM, the elevator opened and Travis' friend stepped out.

Juan was a tall, Hispanic man in his early thirties. Gunther knew instantly by the look in his eyes and the professional way he carried himself that this was a man who knew what he was doing. His well-dressed appearance, neatly trimmed hair, and glasses also added to the man's confident stature. As soon as he exited the elevator, he spotted Gunther and immediately approached him, his expression firm, but not fearful or worried.

"Mr. Lueschen?" he asked, his voice low.

Swallowing hard, Gunther replied, "Juan, it's nice to meet you. Thanks for your–"

The security technician held up a finger to quickly silence the scientist. "Please follow me, Mr. Lueschen," Juan said as he shot a look of warning at Gunther. "We'll get those forms you needed and get you on your way." Turning on his heels, Juan led Gunther back toward the elevator. Once they were inside, Juan placed his thumb on the reader and used his wireless implant to input the code that would allow them access to the upper floors of the building. As the elevator rose, Juan pulled out a handheld device and looked at it with a blank stare for a moment, then tilted it just enough so Gunther could see the words on the screen. DON'T SAY ANYTHING. THERE ARE MICROPHONES AND CAMERAS EVERYWHERE. JUST FOLLOW MY LEAD. Gunther nodded once in acknowledgement, and Juan casually returned the device to his pocket.

The elevator came to a stop and Juan led the way down a hall to one of the plain doors with nothing but a room number to distinguish it from the rest. Juan placed his thumb onto another reader and the door slid open. He stepped into the room with Gunther following close behind. Once they were both inside, the door closed. Sitting down at the lone desk in the room, Juan immediately began communicating wirelessly with the forty-inch computer screen that took up a good portion of the wall. A moment later, he turned his attention back to his guest.

"Please have a seat," he said indicating one of the two other chairs in the room. Gunther sank into the chair gratefully, his nerves already on edge. "Mr. Lueschen, you can relax for now. We're free to talk in here. I've rigged the cameras and microphones in this room personally. I'm afraid you've got some more waiting to do. The building will be closing up to most personnel. Once that's completed, we can proceed with the operation."

Leaning toward the other man, Gunther gave him a look of deep sincerity. "I can't thank you enough for helping me. I don't know how much Travis told you, but my work is. . .is my life. And please, call me Gunther."

Juan gave him a warm smile in return, then his countenance fell. "I'm not going to lie to you. What you're trying to accomplish is very risky. But, if it works and you *are* able to find a way back to earth, you must promise me that you'll come back to get me. I hear that you're doing it so that you can see your wife again. Well, *I'm* doing it for my father. I'm 2nd Generation, but my father never talks much about anything but his dear Espana. He's become somewhat of a hermit in the past several years. If I could get him back to earth, I'm sure he'd snap out of his mental imprisonment. I just want my father back, and I'll do anything to help him."

Gunther actually felt relieved at his words, for now that he knew that Juan had a vested interest in the operation, he felt more secure in trusting him. "I promise that I'll do everything I can to get back to earth, and I promise to come back for you and your family."

"Thank you. I hope you're a man of your word, because it's not like I can hire a hit-man to track you down if you don't keep your promise," Juan said with a grin. Growing more serious, he turned back to his computer screen. "You do realize, of course, that if everything goes as planned, you're still going to have to flee the city. I can cover *my* tracks pretty well, but it's just a matter of time before someone notices something missing and begins an investigation."

"Yeah, I know," he said. "I'm planning on meeting Travis in Dehali. We'll work on the device from there."

"Good. Contact me when it works and I'll meet you there with my family," Juan stated. "Remember, be careful who you trust. Mathison has eyes and ears everywhere. Now, let's go over the plan since we've got some time to kill anyway." As he talked, Juan controlled the images on the screen with commands from his wireless implant. "The basic plan is quite simple. I've changed your identity in the computer. As far as security is concerned, you are Dr. Hamish McGrath. He has all the clearance you'll need. Your thumbprint is now linked to his file. You can wear this white labcoat, and use this satchel to carry the prototype," he said as he handed the items to Gunther. "I'm going to run the cameras on a loop while you're inside the area, so you won't show up on any video."

"What about other workers and staff? Won't they realize that I'm not supposed to be there?" Gunther asked worriedly.

"They might, if you run into them," Juan stated calmly. "However, nearly all of the personnel have gone home, and I naturally know all of the security sweep patterns and who's on night duty. The labcoat alone might be enough to keep the casual observer from bothering you. I'll be monitoring you from here, and if anyone gets close, I'll let you know so you can duck into a side room until they pass. Speaking of which. . ." Juan opened the top drawer of his desk and took out a small earpiece. "I got one of these for you so we could communicate. I've gotta tell ya, if you can afford it, you really need to get some implants. They're *incredibly* useful."

"Actually, I just signed up to get the *Pandora's Box* implant," Gunther replied with a chuckle. "Come to think of it, one way or another I highly doubt I'm going to be able to keep that appointment after tonight." Taking the offered earpiece, Gunther placed it into his right ear.

Once the tiny speaker was in place, Juan's eyes went blank for a second, then he began speaking. "Testing, testing. Can you hear me through the earpiece?"

Gunther looked shocked. "Yes, but. . .I don't see your microphone!"

"It's embedded in my lip," Juan said, pointing at his mouth for emphasis. "These kinds of enhancements come in really handy when I need to communicate with nat-"

The security tech caught himself, but not quick enough. "It's okay. You can say it. 'Naturals'."

"I'm sorry, Gunther. I. . .I didn't mean it in a disrespectful way."

"No offense taken. Just be careful who you say that to," Gunther replied, offering a bit of advice of his own. "Some of us 'naturals' have inferiority complexes. Now, let's get back to the plan. . ."

****

Gunther exited the elevator and strode down the hall doing his best to appear as if he had done this a million times. However, he worried that his shaking hands and perspiring brow would give him away, which only served to fuel his anxiety further. The hallway was deserted, at least for the time being. The possibility that someone would walk around a corner at any given moment kept his heart beating rapidly. Despite Juan's assurances that the area was clear, he still couldn't keep his imagination from drifting down the wrong path.

"Go straight ahead to the first set of double doors," Juan's voice said through the earpiece. "There should be a reader on the right wall."

Here we go, Gunther thought as he approached the reader. *I sure hope Juan knows what he's doing.* Arriving at the doors, he switched the satchel into his left hand and placed his right thumb on the print reader. Without any hesitation, the green light lit up and the door slid open sideways into the wall. Breathing a sigh of relief, Gunther continued on down the hallway.

"Keep going until you pass the next set of elevators," Juan advised. "Stop at the 2nd set of doors on your left and wait for my signal."

Gunther followed his directions once more and waited, his pulse pounding in his ears as he stared nervously around the deserted area. *What am I doing here? I'm getting too old for this! What'll they do to me if they catch me?* Suddenly, bizarre rumors he had heard over the past year about people that had disappeared came to the forefront of his mind, increasing his fear until it was near panic.

"Hey, Gunther. What's wrong?" Juan asked. "You need to pull yourself together. You look so guilty that even a civilian off the street would think you were up to something. You're not going to do your wife any good if you don't get hold of yourself!"

The thought of never seeing Eveleen worked like an antidote to his frazzled nerves. Taking a deep breath, Gunther closed his eyes and forced himself to relax. A second later, Juan's voice spoke again. "Keep your focus. 'Be strong and courageous. Do not fear or be afraid. For I am with you.'"

Gunther frowned at the reference. He didn't know enough about Juan to know where the quote was from, but he somehow found it encouraging. He continued to follow Juan's directions without incident for several more minutes until he finally arrived at his destination.

The final set of doors opened, and Gunther entered the lab. As soon as he stepped inside, the lights in the room came on. Although the layout was slightly different, the room had a strong resemblance to the lab in which he and his colleagues had used to develop the Portal Stabilizer. There were several tables surrounded by stools in the center of the floor and along the walls. Above the workstations were cabinets and shelves containing various items, books, and other materials. Nearly the entire length of the wall opposite the door consisted of several large windows made of thick glass that looked into an adjoining room. Inside this other room was an object that, though much smaller in size, looked strikingly similar to the Portal Stabilizer.

Only it was in the unmistakable form of a rifle.

Neither Juan nor Travis were able to find out what the weapon did, but if it had something to do with particle physics and Gunther's own research, then he was truly frightened to imagine what would come out of the end of that nozzle.

"Forget about the weapon and go get what you came for," Juan said, drawing Gunther's focus back to the task at hand. "There's a manual computer terminal with a reader attached to it on your left. Hurry up and find the data you're looking for. No one is in your vicinity at the moment, but I wouldn't push our luck."

Crossing over to the computer, Gunther placed his thumb against the reader, causing the machine to spring to life. After successfully navigating past the passwords and security features, with Juan's assistance, he started to work. It took him several nerve-wracking minutes to find any reference to the Portal Stabilizer. Finally, his searching paid off as he discovered a file called, "Vortex Weapon." Opening it quickly, he scanned the headings of the files. Satisfied that he had found what he came for, he started downloading the information onto his storage drive.

"Uh oh. Don't freak out, Gunther, I've got this under control. But you're about to have company," Juan said calmly.

"What?" Gunther asked aloud, his head snapping up to search frantically around the room for signs that someone was approaching. "Where?"

Hearing the panic in his voice, Juan responded quickly, "Relax. You've still got a minute or so. Just calmly walk over to the storage room where your Portal device should be stored. You can wait in there until the guards have left the area."

"But what about the mini drive? It's not finished loading yet!" Gunther asked loudly.

"Keep your voice down!" Juan chastised. "Don't you remember what I told you? They might hear your voice. Forget about the drive right now. Get into the storage area!"

Turning around, Gunther headed for the storage room. In his haste and nervousness, he accidently bumped into one of the worktables. Under normal circumstances, the scraping sound it made wouldn't have been very loud. But to Gunther's heightened senses, it sounded like a blazing siren. Cursing himself for his clumsiness, he continued moving toward the door. Outside the room, he could begin to hear the sound of booted feet approaching, accompanied by muffled voices. After a moment of fumbling with the print reader, the door finally opened and he slipped inside. The motion detector in the storage room immediately turned the lights on, causing Gunther to frantically search for the manual switch. Mere seconds after he finally managed to turn the lights off, he heard the double doors leading into the lab open.

Panic threatened to overwhelm him as he huddled in the darkened room, the filtered light from the lab streaming in through the small window set into the door. Gunther strained to hear what the voices were saying.

"Stay calm," Juan said, the sudden voice startling Gunther. "There are two night guards checking out the room. They don't seem to be on alert, just curious as to why the lights were on. They should be leaving any minute."

Closing his eyes, Gunther waged a silent war inside himself against his own fear. After what seemed like an eternity, he heard the men leave the room. "Just stay where you are for a second. Let's make sure they're really gone." Finally confident that the men were not going to bother them further, Juan said, "Okay. They've left. Let's finish this and get you out of there."

Still shaking, Gunther turned on the light and froze. In his excitement to escape detection from the guards, he hadn't noticed that the room in which he had entered was empty of everything except boxes and a few loose items on some shelves. A sickening feeling roiled around in Gunther's stomach. "Juan. . .I. . .I thought you said that the prototype of the stabilizer would be in this storage room! But it's not here!"

After several seconds of silence, Juan's voice reappeared. "Someone must have moved it without updating the inventory log. I. . .I'm sorry, Gunther. It was supposed to have been there."

"So what do we do now?" the scientist asked in exasperation.

"You're just going to have to take the data and run," Juan retorted. "I don't know what else to say."

Leaving the storage room, Gunther's gaze was drawn back to the weapon in the next room. Making up his mind, he ran over to the door leading into the room and pressed his thumb to the reader. "What are you doing?" Juan asked. Despite the fact that his voice was being transmitted through an earpiece, Gunther could clearly hear his concern.

"If I can't use the prototype, maybe I can reconfigure the weapon. As long as the design is similar, it might work," he replied as he stepped into the room and removed the device from its mounting atop a sturdy tripod. Opening the satchel hanging around his shoulder, he set the weapon inside, then zipped it back up.

"I'm not sure that's a good idea," Juan said. "The scientists that work in this lab will recognize that the weapon is missing a lot quicker than they would notice the absence of the prototype."

"I know, but I've got to take that chance," Gunther said with resolve. His prize secured, he ran back into the main room and headed over to the computer. Noting that the device had finished transferring the data, he ejected it and stuffed it into his pants pocket. Then, just as he was about to power down the computer, he remembered Travis's mistake. Going into the program history, he erased any traces that he had been there. However, as he was doing so, another file name caught his attention. Opening it up, he began to read.

An acute sense of dread and fear spread throughout every inch of his body as he digested the words on the screen. With his hands shaking so badly he could barely function, he reinserted the storage device and downloaded the new file. "Juan, you. . .you won't. . .I can't believe. . .you've got to. . .to come with me."

Silence was the only reply.

"Juan?" Gunther whispered. "Juan, are you there?"

Suddenly, the doors to his left burst open as two guards entered, their laser rifles pointed directly at Gunther.

Chapter 9

Escaping the Compound

*B*oth guards were dressed in sleek, dark grey military uniforms with matching hats that covered their short cropped hair and shielded their face with a front bill. The only difference between the two men was that one appeared to be in his thirties, while the other looked fresh out of the academy.

"Freeze!" the older of the two commanded, while the younger one surveyed the room in search of any other intruders. His search completed, he approached Gunther and proceeded to bind his hands behind his back.

Caught and alone, Gunther felt his knees give out from beneath him. He slumped to the floor, his mind going numb from prolonged and intense fear. Lying on the floor, Gunther barely registered the fact that the older guard had ejected his mini drive and placed it in a shirt pocket. To his addled mind, the men's voices seemed distant; their conversation broken and disjointed.

". . .captain wants to know what's in the bag. Search it."

". . .some sort of weapon."

". . .check the other room. Is there a tripod?"

". . .must be the same one."

Gunther could see that the two men each had a wireless implant, and from time to time they paused to communicate silently with someone else. Shutting out the present, he began to reflect upon what he had read moments before. In his delirious state, he began mumbling aloud. "They don't even know. . .being deceived. . .only a matter of time. . .someone must tell them. . ."

The older of the two guards narrowed his eyes and knelt next to Gunther while his partner continued to communicate wirelessly. With the guard in close proximity, Gunther's eyes turned their focus to the man. "Please, you don't understand. People have to be warned! I can. . .I can reverse the portals! We can get back to earth if only. . ."

As his words trailed off, the guard stood and looked to his partner, who had just finished his conversation. The two men spoke briefly, their words filling Gunther with trepidation and fear. "Captain Hubing said that his superiors want us to. . .to eliminate the intruder and remove all evidence of the disturbance," the older guard said. Looking up once more at the man's partner, Gunther could tell that although he was somewhat disturbed by the orders, his face showed the resolve necessary to carry them out. The older man's face was devoid of emotion, leaving Gunther little doubt as to his fate.

With his mind growing increasingly numb to his physical surroundings, Gunther was completely unprepared for what happened next. As the younger guard reached over to pull Gunther to his feet, he suddenly tripped unexpectedly and fell to the ground. The older guard, moving incredibly fast, jumped on top of the two of them. At nearly the same moment, two short bursts from a laser pistol flashed past Gunther's head, causing a small explosion as the beams struck the ceiling. A split second later, a third shot rang out, but no visible light was seen.

"I need you to do exactly as I say if you want to live. There's no time for questions. Do you understand?"

It took Gunther's confused brain several seconds to realize that the words had been spoken by the guard who had landed on top of him. Even before Gunther nodded his assent, he felt the pressure of the man's body on his back lessen. As Gunther rose awkwardly to his feet, he felt the guard remove the bindings from his wrists. That accomplished, the guard's eyes became blank as he communicated with his superiors.

Finishing his conversation, he looked back at Gunther. "Take off your lab coat. Quickly," he commanded, his voice barely audible. Doing as instructed, Gunther removed his coat, noting as he did so that the man had begun removing his fallen partner's military jacket, utility belt and hat. Once they had both finished their tasks, the guard exchanged the items for the lab coat. "Put these on," he said as he proceeded to wrap the lab coat around his partner's head and torso. "Your pants aren't the same color, but they're dark enough to not be too obvious."

"It's too small," Gunther whispered, pulling at the jacket in hopes that he could make it meet in the middle.

"It'll have to do," the man said quietly as he unzipped his own jacket to match Gunther's. Pointing at the unconscious body of the younger man, he spoke, the volume of his voice returning to normal. "Okay, Nick, grab the feet and let's put him on the cart. Once we've disposed of this, we can return to clean up." Grabbing the indicated cart, the guard proceeded to transfer the items from it onto one of the tables, then rolled it over to where the other guard's body lay.

Grabbing the man's feet, Gunther breathed a sigh of relief as the man moved slightly, indicating that he wasn't dead, but merely unconscious. On the count of three, the two men heaved the body onto the cart. Reaching down, Gunther's rescuer grabbed the satchel containing the Vortex weapon and placed it on the bottom shelf of the cart.

Moving up next to Gunther, he whispered, "I shot the camera in this room, so the other security personnel won't be able to see our actions. But when we leave this room, keep your head down so the cameras can't get a good look at your face. If we meet anyone, just pretend that you have a headache and keep looking down. Don't say a word, or the microphones will detect your voice. I'm sure I don't need to tell you what'll happen if we're caught." Without waiting for any indication that Gunther had heard him, he lead the way out of the room. After a moment's hesitation, Gunther grabbed the cart and headed toward the exit.

As they walked down the hall, Gunther's mind finally caught up to his circumstances. Numerous questions began to invade his consciousness. *Who is this man? Why would a government security guard risk his life to help me? Can I trust him? What if he's leading me further into an elaborate trap? Maybe he's trying to use me to catch Juan.* Pushing the thoughts to the back of his mind, he focused solely on his immediate predicament.

The guard guided the two of them through a maze of corridors, passed several doors and into an elevator. All the while, Gunther followed behind pushing the cart, his knuckles white on the handle. They didn't encounter anyone until they stepped off of the elevator and into a maintenance hallway several floors down. Waiting for them only ten feet away was another man in a military uniform, the decorations on his shoulders indicating he was of a higher rank than Gunther's rescuer.

The sight of the newcomer sent a fresh wave of fear coursing through Gunther's veins, causing him to grip the edge of the cart even tighter to prevent his hands from shaking. Despite his best efforts, however, he couldn't keep his arms or legs from trembling as his new companion stepped closer to his superior.

"Lewis, Szulcewski, it's about time you two arrived," the man said, his face firm and businesslike as he glanced at the unmoving body on the cart. Gunther's heart beat painfully in his chest as Braedon's superior glanced momentarily at him. Keeping his head down, Gunther held his breath, waiting for some sign that he had been discovered and wondering what he would do if that happened.

"Sorry, Captain Hubing," Braedon replied. "We got here as fast as we could."

"Commisioner Holst is furious. He's ordered us to investigate this security breach, but he also needs us to keep it quiet," The Captain said, his irritation obvious. "Once the two of you finish cleaning up this mess, report to me for debriefing."

"Yes, sir. Did they find the mole?" Braedon asked.

"Not yet," Hubing replied. "Whoever was sending the signal was good at covering himself. Until Security finds him, the building is locked down tight, including the exit you're planning to use. So, I've come down here to personally talk to Riggs and Walker. Once they're out of the way, you can proceed. I don't want them to know more than necessary."

Gunther was relieved to hear that Juan had not been caught, but still worried that he would be found out. *If he's captured, what will happen to his family?* Gunther wondered as he kept walking.

After they had travelled down two more halls, the captain stopped them at a set of doors. "Wait here," he said. Glancing over at Gunther, he noted that his head was still down and frowned. "Szulcewski, what's wrong with you?" Forgetting himself, Gunther glanced up at the man, their eyes meeting for a split second. But even that instant was long enough for the man to realize the truth. Surprise registering on his face, Captain Hubing reached for his weapon. However, before his fingers could wrap themselves around the grip, Braedon sprang into action. Grabbing his superior's arm, Braedon spun him around and used the momentum to slam him up against the wall. The impact knocked the man unconscious and he slumped to the ground.

"C'mon, we're almost out," Braedon said as he resumed his place at the front of the cart.

"But. . .but what are you g. . .going to do, just leave him lying here?" Gunther asked, his voice trembling. "And what about the guards? Now that we don't have *him* to move the guards out of our way, how will we get past them?"

"Leave that to me," Braedon replied. "Just keep going!"

Having no other choice, Gunther swallowed any further questions and lowered his head as Braedon opened the door and headed toward the exit. As soon as Braedon and Gunther stepped into the hallway, the two men watching the door pointed their rifles in their direction. However, the moment they recognized Braedon, they lowered their weapons and relaxed somewhat until they noticed the body in the cart.

"Hey, Braedon, what's going on?" the first man asked, his face alert but confused.

"There was a break-in," Braedon replied. "This guy tried to steal some data from one of the labs. Unfortunately for him, the security techs tracked him down and sent us to deal with him."

The men exchanged glances as Gunther and Braedon drew closer. With the discovery by the captain still fresh in his mind, Gunther knew it would just be a matter of time before these two realized that he wasn't who he pretended to be. He only hoped that whatever Braedon had in mind would be enough.

"Poor schmuck," the second guard snickered. "Who'd be crazy enough to try to break into here?"

"Yeah, I know. Right?" Braedon agreed with a winning smile. "Well, the Captain ordered us to dispose of the body. So, if you'll excuse us. . ."

"Wait a sec," the first guard held up a hand. "We've just got to confirm it with the Captain."

Just as the man's eyes lost their focus to indicate a transmission via his wireless implant, Braedon closed the distance between them and attacked. In all of his years, Gunther had never seen anyone move so fast. In less than a second, Braedon had rendered the first man unconscious and had turned to face the second. Caught by surprise, the second guard barely reacted in time to ward off the first of Braedon's blows. Backpedaling frantically, the man raised his rifle toward his attacker. With a swift high kick, Gunther's companion knocked the weapon out of the man's hand. Taking advantage of his opponent's shock, Braedon crouched down and cut the legs out from underneath him with a sweep of his leg. Then, before the man could recover, Braedon knocked him unconscious with a quick punch.

"We're out of time!" Braedon said hurriedly. "Forget the cart. Let's move!" Reaching under the cart, he grabbed the satchel containing the Vortex weapon and headed toward the doors. Placing his thumb onto the reader, he bolted through the exit the second it opened, not even looking to see if his companion was following.

The two men sprinted outside into a loading area, their eyes searching everywhere in the dim light for signs of attackers. The bluish 'moonlight' from the Globe far above created eerie shadows everywhere. Suddenly, the loading dock was illuminated by the headlights of an approaching vehicle! Startled, Gunther let out a small cry of fear as the vehicle came to a stop a couple of feet in front of them. Turning toward the physicist, Braedon placed a hand on his shoulder. "They're friendly. C'mon! Get in!"

Immediately, the back door of the hovering vehicle popped open. Braedon cast a quick glance over his shoulder as he shoved Gunther toward the open door. The two men dove into the back of the hovercar, and Braedon slammed the door shut.

"Go!" he commanded.

The driver spun the vehicle around one hundred and eighty degrees, then hit the accelerator. However, before the hovercar could clear the edge of the building, Braedon pointed and called out a warning. "Left wall! Look out!"

Gunther could barely make out the shape of a man clinging to the wall before the shape detached itself and fell to the street. The figure stood directly in their path, seemingly unafraid of the approaching vehicle.

"I knew it," Braedon breathed in concern.

"What. . .what is it?" the driver asked, the words getting stuck in his throat.

"A Guardian!"

Chapter 10

The Guardian

"Ram him!" Braedon called out to the driver. Whether due to Braedon's command or his own fear, the driver immediately hit the accelerator, causing the vehicle to speed toward the Guardian standing in the middle of the road.

Not wanting to look, yet unable to turn his gaze away, Gunther watched as the hovercar quickly closed the gap between itself and the black-clad soldier. Then, impossibly, the technologically altered human did a backflip and landed onto the hood of the speeding vehicle. Based on the velocity of their car, Gunther expected the man to slide off. However, as soon as the Guardian landed on his knees, he spread his arms out wide and stuck in place, almost as if he had been glued down. It was only then that Gunther remembered what Travis had told him about the special suits that had been engineered for the Guardians – suits based on the sticking capacity of geckos' feet. With a wirelessly transmitted mental command, the Guardian could change the texture of the suit from a hard, rubber-like substance that served as armor, to the soft, flexible, micro-suction cups that allowed them to climb walls and stick to surfaces.

The three men in the vehicle watched in momentary shock as the Guardian rolled his arms in an upward motion,

releasing the suction of the suit from the hood and reposi-
tioning his arms into an upright stance. Once stable, the
helmeted head snapped up to look at the occupants of the
vehicle. Although the black, V-shaped visor covered the man's
entire face, Gunther imagined he could feel his gaze boring
into him. Like all Type 1 Guardians, the man was chosen for
his physical size and strength. The tight-fitting, solid black suit
clung to the man's body, accentuating his bulging muscles and
lean physique. Gunther wondered if Braedon's skill and speed
would be able to defeat this technologically altered soldier if
the battle boiled down to a hand-to-hand fight.

Coming to his senses, the driver began swerving the
car slightly until they finally cleared the end of the alleyway.
The movement of the vehicle kept the Guardian focused on
keeping his balance and prevented him from firing his wrist
mounted laser gun into the vehicle.

"Keep him off balance," Braedon commanded as he
climbed halfway out of the window. Using his right arm to
keep his own balance stable, Braedon began firing with his
laser pistol. The first couple of shots went wide of their target
as the motion of the hovercar threw off his aim. Although
the Guardian's suit allowed him to stick to the car, the driver's
erratic swerving caused him to spend all of his energy just to
stay atop the hood, allowing Braedon the time he needed to
perfect his aim. Due to the fact that the man's suit was in its
softer form, the lasers tore large holes into the Guardian's right
shoulder.

Reacting to the attack, the Guardian lifted his right hand
off of the hood and began firing back at Braedon. The driver
continued to swerve, doing his best to make forward progress down the mostly empty street, avoid obstacles and other
cars, and shake the attacker all at the same time. Although the
Guardian could not be shaken from his perch, the driver's
attempts served to keep the man's computer-enhanced brain
from hitting his target.

"Hang on!" the driver suddenly shouted, causing Braedon and Gunther to both grab onto the seats in front of them. Immediately, the driver slammed on the breaks and turned the wheel. The change in speed and direction caught the Guardian by surprise. With the suit still attached to the hood at the knees and left hand, the man's body bent awkwardly backwards. Had he been a normal human, his bones would have snapped. However, with his enhanced strength, the move served only to render him momentarily helpless.

"We've got to figure out how to get him off the hood!" the driver yelled out as he once again hit the accelerator, sending the vehicle lurching forward. The man's words penetrated the fog that had surrounded Gunther's mind. Remembering what Travis had once told him about the weaknesses of the Guardian's suits, Gunther looked around the car for anything that might help. Catching sight of the bottle of water in the front cup holder, Gunther dove into the front seat and grabbed it.

"What are you doing?" the driver said angrily as Gunther righted himself and began unscrewing the lid. Ignoring the man's question, Gunther reached out the window and poured the liquid onto the hood just as the Guardian set his gloved hand down to renew his grip. However, the moment the suit hit the water, the driver understood Gunther's actions. Gripping the wheel tighter in his hands, he swerved hard to the right, causing the Guardian's weight to shift onto the now slippery hand. After several more attempts to dislodge their attacker by swerving, the water managed to loosen the suit's hold enough for the driver to fling the man from the hood.

As his armored body hit the pavement, Braedon and Gunther spun their heads around to see what had become of their attacker. "Get us out of here quick, Jace!" Braedon said. "He's getting up!"

To Gunther's surprise, the Guardian quickly jumped to his feet as if nothing out of the ordinary had occurred and began running toward them.

"I'm trying," Jace shot back. "But I just ran into a batch of late night traffic! Why is it in the holovids there's always enough room to swerve around the other vehicles! We're stuck behind a truck and two cars, and unless you want me to crash headlong into the oncoming row of traffic, we're just going to have to wait a second for an opening!"

"Push the cars in front of us, then!" Braedon called out. "That Guardian's coming up fast!"

Sure enough, Gunther could see the technologically-enhanced soldier running faster than any normal man he had ever seen. In another few seconds, he would be on top of them. Several blasts from Braedon's weapon flew toward the Guardian. However, instead of diving out of the way of the shots, the armored man simply raised his arm and blocked the shots.

"The suit has changed into its armored form," Gunther advised. "Combined with the metal lacing the skin on his arm and his enhanced reflexes, your shots will never do him much damage!"

"I'm aware of that!" Braedon said through gritted teeth as he kept firing. "But by focusing on deflecting my shots, he can't concentrate on running. It also keeps him off balance, hopefully buying us the time we need to escape!"

Jace, finally able to push past the cars in front of them, hit the accelerator. Seeing his prey escaping, the Guardian put all of his energy into running. The man's enhanced leg muscles, combined with his ability to cut corners and fit through spaces too tight for his target, allowed him to keep up with the hovercar. Braedon continued his barrage of blaster fire, but due to Jace's maneuvering, none of his shots hit home.

Meanwhile, Gunther watched helplessly in the front seat as Jace swerved in an out of traffic. "Where are we going?" he asked the driver. For the first time, Gunther got a good look at the man. He was young, perhaps in his early twenties, dark skinned, and wore his hair cut short. Across his neck was a nasty scar perhaps three inches long. He was dressed in plain jeans and a dark green T-shirt.

With his concentration focused on driving, Jace didn't immediately answer. "I'm trying to lose this guy while at the same time get us to someplace where we can hide. It won't be long before the rest of the police are onto us. If that happens, we're gonners."

Gunther was about to ask another question, but the sudden appearance of a large truck coming out of a cross street halted any further conversation. "Look out!" he managed to yell. Seeing the truck at the last second, Jace yanked the wheel hard to the right, avoiding a full sideways collision. However, the sudden turn sent them careening wildly out of control. To his credit, Jace was able to avoid a major accident. However, in doing so the corner of the hovercar hit the edge of a parked van. The resulting impact spun the hovercar sideways, bringing it to a full stop.

"Everyone alright?" Braedon asked, his own senses slightly rattled. Both Jace and Gunther replied in the affirmative. Suddenly, a laser blast flew past the hood of the car, barely missing it and colliding with a nearby building. Turning to look in the direction from which the shot originated, Braedon could see the Guardian running full tilt down the street, closing the distance between them rapidly.

"Jace, get us OUT OF HERE!" Braedon yelled as he began firing his own laser pistol once again.

Fearing that their chance of escaping would soon be gone, Jace slammed on the accelerator, catapulting them down the street. However, before they had gone more than one hundred feet, a second laser blast struck the back window. Braedon immediately ducked down to protect himself as shards of reinforced duraglass flew in all directions. Next to him, Gunther heard Jace cry out in pain as several pieces cut his neck and face.

The intense wave of pain from the glass caused Jace to miscalculate as he tried to turn right into an alleyway. Gunther let out a cry of alarm as they slid sideways into the edge of a building. The car shuddered as it came to a stop once more. This time, however, before any of the men could recover from the crash, another laser blast hit the back of the vehicle, causing the gravity control units to fail. The hovercar dropped heavily to the ground with a deep thud.

Stunned by the turn of events, Gunther was surprised when a hand grabbed his shoulder and pulled him into an upright position. "Can you run?" Still shook up, it took him a moment to realize that it was Braedon who asked the question. "Yes. . .yes I. . .I think so."

"Then let's go!" he commanded as he kicked open the back door of the car. Jumping out, he threw the satchel containing the vortex weapon around his head and shoulder, then started firing his weapon once more at the still approaching Guardian. As soon as Gunther had extricated himself from the vehicle, Braedon stopped firing, grabbed him by the arm and began running down the darkened alley. Gunther fought hard to keep from tripping over the debris that lay hidden in the deep shadows created by the diffused bluish light that emanated from the Globe.

"What. . .about. . .Jace?" Gunther asked as they ran, his breathing already heavy from the unexpected exercise.

"He'll be okay once we're gone," Braedon replied as he continually glanced over his shoulder. "The Guardian doesn't care about him. He's after us."

"But, where. . .are. . .we going?"

Before Braedon could answer, the Guardian appeared at the entrance to the alley not more than fifty feet behind them. "Keep running!" Braedon urged as he paused to take several shots at their pursuer.

Although he knew they could never outrun the technologically enhanced soldier, Gunther continued moving as fast as his out of shape body would carry him. Risking a glance behind him, he watched in horror as the Guardian sprinted toward Braedon, blocking the laser blasts with uncanny precision. Feeling helpless, Gunther watched as Braedon threw down his weapon and the satchel and moved into a martial arts ready position. Not knowing what else to do, Gunther ducked behind a garbage bin and stared in amazement as the two combatants collided.

Although the Guardian was slightly bigger, Braedon still used his impressive six-foot one-inch frame to its fullest advantage. Unable to match the man's strength, Braedon moved in close to his attacker and attempted to throw him off balance. Ducking under the man's punch, Braedon used his right arm to push against the Guardian's chest while simultaneously kicking his leg out from under him. Off balance, the armored soldier crashed to the ground. Taking advantage of his opponent's weakness, Braedon struck out at the man's neck.

Despite his impressive efforts, Braedon's blows didn't seem to have any effect on the man. Knowing he was outmatched, Braedon dodged several kicks and punches and spun away from him. As he did so, Gunther suddenly remembered the satchel and the Vortex weapon contained within it. Gathering his courage, he bolted out from his hiding place.

Braedon, catching on to his companion's intent, tried to distract his adversary. The Guardian regained his footing and moved toward Braedon, his back to Gunther. Braedon dove in once more toward his opponent, but this time the Guardian anticipated the move. With one swift blow to the side of his head, the Guardian rendered him unconscious. Turning, the man faced Gunther. Despite the faceless mask, Gunther could sense a moment of hesitation.

That hesitation cost him his prize. For at that moment, a blast of electricity suddenly lit up the darkness and struck the Guardian. The enhanced soldier stood immobile for a moment, then collapsed to the ground.

Stunned by the turn of events, Gunther stared in shock as a man appeared from out of the darkness, a large weapon held in his hands and pointed straight in his direction.

Chapter 11

Crimson Liberty

"We must move quickly," the man said as he ran over to where Braedon lay on the ground. "The Volt's effects won't keep the Guardian down for long."

Gunther studied his rescuer for a moment as he tried to calm his pounding heart. He was a dark skinned man with a clean-shaven head, black mustache and goatee. Based on the wrinkles in his forehead and around his eyes, Gunther guessed that the two of them were about the same age. He was dressed in all black, except for a cloak made of a strange material that he wore around his shoulders. As he moved, the cloak's appearance changed, causing him to nearly disappear into his surroundings. The disorienting sensation was made worse by the dim, bluish light from the Globe that cast deep shadows around the alley.

Setting his weapon down on the ground, the man pulled out a small item from a pocket, then knelt down beside Braedon and placed the item near his nose. A moment later, Braedon began to stir. The man's gaze swept the alley in all directions as he helped Braedon to sit up. Although the man remained calm, Gunther could tell by his expression that he feared they would be discovered at any moment.

"Braedon, we need to move," he said, his voice deep and resonant. "The Guardian's computer systems will reboot in a minute or two, and the Volt takes longer than that to charge. Can you walk?"

Staring up at the man, Gunther saw Braedon's face soften in recognition. "Master Sergeant Russell! Thank God."

Helping him to his feet, the man frowned. "How many times do I have to tell you? I gave up that title long ago."

Braedon smiled, in spite of still being in obvious pain from the Guardian's blow. "Sorry. Calling you 'Steven' still seems so awkward to me."

Leaving Braedon to stand on his own, Steven grabbed two items from near the wall. "Here. Put this on. We've got to get out of here before. . ." The distant sound of sirens filled the air, adding urgency to his words.

Not needing any further prompting, Braedon grabbed one of the items, which turned out to be another cloak identical to the one Steven wore, and threw it around his shoulders. While he did so, Steven reached into another pocket and withdrew several small, round devices and began attaching two each to Braedon's chest, waist, knees, and finally his forehead. Without any further explanation, Steven motioned to Gunther to step closer while Braedon picked up the satchel containing the Vortex weapon. Grabbing the last of the cloaks, Steven placed it around Gunther's shoulders and repeated the process of placing the devices on his body in the same locations.

"What are these for?" Gunther asked as he studied the strange material of the cloak.

"They are mini cameras," Steven replied. "The images they capture are projected onto the back of the cloak. If you stand still or move very slowly, you will effectively become invisible. It's extremely useful under poor lighting conditions. Since you won't be able to see me, follow my verbal cues." Retrieving his weapon, Steven grabbed the hood of the cloak and pulled it over his head, indicating for the others to do the same. Once they were ready, Steven led the way and sprinted down the alley away from the damaged hovercar.

"What about Jace?" Braedon asked as the three men ran. "We can't just leave him!"

"Don't worry. Cameron helped him escape," Steven said in a hushed tone. "We'll meet up with them later. Now, we're nearing the end of the alley. Slow down to walking speed and keep your body facing the wall, including your head. All of the cameras must face the same direction for the effect to work. When you reach the corner, turn your body quickly so that you stay parallel with the wall."

Steven led the way and was the first to round the corner. After a moment, he called quietly for Braedon to follow. Although it was only a few seconds before Steven urged Gunther to proceed, the ever-increasing volume of the approaching sirens made the time seem to stretch forever. When the time came for him to move, he felt as if every pair of eyes within a mile must be focused in his direction. Having his back to the street turned out to be not only disconcerting, but very disorienting. He fought with every ounce of his will to keep from turning his head to see behind him. Only Steven's muffled voice beside him kept him from doing so.

"We're almost there," Steven said from somewhere to Gunther's left. "Just keep following the wall a few more feet, then turn another corner." The three cloaked men proceeded around the new corner in the same fashion as before. Finally, after several more torturous seconds, Steven gave them permission to remove their cloaks.

Taking in their surroundings, Gunther noted with relief that they were in another darkened alley nearly a full block away from the original scene of the confrontation. Steven quickly instructed them to remove the miniature cameras and place them, as well as Braedon and Gunther's cloaks, inside the satchel along with the Vortex weapon. Taking his own cloak, Steven wrapped the Volt rifle in it, and tucked it under his arm.

A block away, a crowd had now gathered in the streets, causing the newly arrived police officers to spend their first several minutes on the scene corralling the spectators. With their attention thus diverted, the officers never saw the three darkly clad men stroll casually out of another alley and walk away from the area.

****

Once they had walked far enough so that they could no longer hear the sound of the commotion, Gunther found himself begin to relax for the first time that day. He had done it! He had succeeded in retrieving the data that would hopefully allow him to successfully stabilize a portal and return to Earth. And even though he hadn't been able to get the original prototype of the Stabilizer, he felt that there was a strong chance he could either build another one using the data, or he could at least use parts of the Vortex weapon, if not the whole device, to accomplish his goal. For the first time since arriving in Elysium, Gunther felt a real sense of hope.

Provided, of course, that he could trust his new 'friends'.

"So, where are we going now?" Gunther asked as Steven led them into a residential section of the city. Based on the distance the Globe had travelled along its track, Gunther guessed the time to be somewhere near one thirty in the morning.

"There's a safehouse nearby," Steven replied as he led them past several homes. "We'll spend the night there."

Not knowing whether it was due to the fact that he was walking down an unknown street far from his normal area of residency very early in the morning or from some sixth sense, but Gunther felt a bit of unease settle in his chest. He still wasn't sure if he could trust these men, but at the same time, he knew he didn't have any other choice. *They did get me out of the Research and Records compound and rescue me from the Guardian, but still. . .what do they want? Why did they help me? What if they turn out to be criminals. . .or worse?* Studying the men more carefully, Gunther felt a new sense of calm settle over him. *No. There's something about their eyes. . .something about the way that Braedon looked at Steven when he saw him in the alley. There's a story here, but one thing seems sure: they're not criminals.*

Steven led them to the back door of a small, but decent-looking house with a well- manicured lawn and wooden fence. Glancing around one last time, Steven placed his thumb on the reader and opened the door. Once they were all inside, he closed it again and led the other two men down a set of stairs into a well-furnished basement. He lit a single lamp, then urged the other men to sit on one of the pieces of plush furniture.

Braedon and Gunther sank heavily onto the couch and arm chair, the soft cushions kneading the tension from the evening's activities out of their bodies. While the two of them relaxed, Steven reached into the freezer section of a nearby refrigerator and withdrew an ice pack. He handed it to Braedon, who gratefully accepted it and placed it against the side of his head to ease the swelling from the Guardian's blow. Reaching back into the refrigerator, Steven pulled out three bottles of cold water. Tossing one to each of his companions, he opened the third, took a huge drink, and sat down on a wooden chair facing Gunther.

"Now that we're no longer trying to evade capture, let me formally introduce myself," Steven began as he offered his hand to Gunther. "I'm Steven Russell, 3rd Gen. Nice to meet you."

Gunther, warmed by the man's hospitality and politeness, shook his hand. "Gunther Lueschen, 1st Gen, 197. Thank you for saving us back there. And thank you for saving me back in the lab, not to mention getting me out of there," he said, directing his comments at Braedon. "I owe you my life."

Sitting forward, Braedon offered his hand to Gunther as well. "You're most welcome," he said. "I suppose we should also officially introduce ourselves. I'm Braedon Lewis, 1st Gen 192."

With the introductions complete, Steven sat back in his chair. "I'm sure you both are exhausted and would like to get some sleep, but I think you'll agree that we've got some important issues to discuss and one amazing story to tell. Mr. Lueschen, if I were in your shoes, I'd be wondering exactly who we are and why we helped you. So, to put you at ease, let me start by saying that we will *not* harm you in any way. However, until we know more about you, we're not at liberty to tell you much more about ourselves. I hope you understand."

Comforted by the man's words, Gunther nodded. "Thank you. I. . .I guess that's about the best I can hope for. After all, it seems only fair that since you saved my life, I should be the one to share my information first. At the same time, I also trust that you will understand if I don't share all of the details of my story, as I need to protect the identities of those who helped me."

With that, Gunther launched into an account of how and why he entered the lab, leaving out the names of Travis and Juan from the narrative. Steven and Braedon exchanged glances at the mention of the possibility of finding a way to stabilize the portals, yet seemed unsurprised by the existence of the Vortex weapon.

Once Gunther had finished, Steven glanced at Braedon, then returned his gaze to his guest. "Mr. Lueschen, before Braedon begins his explanation, let me first say that you may be the answer to years of prayers. If there is even a *chance* that you can get the portals stabilized, then I can promise you that you will have the full backing of our entire organization at your disposal."

"Organization?" Gunther asked, somewhat taken aback by Steven's serious demeanor.

"Yes. Braedon and I both belong to Crimson Liberty."

At the mention of the name, Gunther stiffened, his apprehension rekindled. Noting his reaction, Steven frowned. "I see our 'reputation' precedes us," he said, his voice full of frustration.

"But. . .but you're a. . .a religious terrorist organization," Gunther stammered in confusion.

"I see you've been listening to the media," Braedon commented. "All of the news feeds are under the control of Mathison's government, and as you've witnessed first hand, the government isn't the most reliable source of information. They tell the people what they want the people to hear. They don't like what we stand for, so they paint us as an extremist group and blame all sorts of atrocities on us. In the war of appearances, they certainly have the upper hand."

"If you're not a terrorist organization, then what *do* you stand for?" Gunther said, somewhat apprehensive.

"I'm glad you asked," Steven said. "Too often people only hear what we're *against* instead of what we're *for*. We believe that *all* men and women are created equal by God, that *all* life is precious, and that *all* of mankind should be allowed to live out their faith in public without fear of government reprisal."

Gunther's frown deepened. "That all sounds reasonable. Why would the government label you as a terrorist organization?"

"Because as you've seen, the government has an agenda," Steven stated. "They're not just content with building roads and keeping the peace. Since taking office nearly ten years ago, Mathison has been pushing legislation after legislation through the congress that has slowly been eroding our freedoms. And, of course, it was all in the name of preserving the 'jewel that is Elysium.' Your story is a perfect example. The government *knew* that you and your team had found a way to possibly stabilize the portals. But rather than continue to develop that technology, they converted it into a weapon, or weapons."

"Mr. Lueschen–" Braedon began.

"Please, call me Gunther," he interjected.

Nodding in agreement, Braedon continued. "You're 1st Gen, right? You said you arrived in 197, so you lived most of your life on Earth. Mathison is showing the same kind of mentality that Hitler showed just prior to World War II. If he is allowed to continue down this path, there'll soon be no way to stop him. There's a famous quote from a Lutheran pastor named Martin Niemoller who lived at that time. He said, 'When they came for the Jews, I did nothing, for I am not a Jew. When they came for the Socialists, I did nothing, for I am not a Socialist. When they came for the labor leaders, the homosexuals, the gypsies, I did nothing, for I am none of these, and when they came for me, I was alone, there was no one to stand up for me.'"

Steven looked at Gunther intensely as he picked up where Braedon left off. "With that quote in mind, many of us in Crimson Liberty *have* been speaking out against Mathison's policies for years, often at a heavy price." The way he said the last phrase, Gunther knew that Steven was speaking of his own experience. Although he wanted to ask about it, Gunther felt it would be best to save the question for later and allow his host to continue. "Several of us tried to convince the public that in order for a society to be free, dissent must be tolerated in the public square. Our message was mostly rejected, and we were labeled as 'bigots' and 'intolerant' by the media and social elites. Even many in our own churches didn't listen to us, and, unfortunately, our words turned out to be frighteningly prophetic."

"How so?" Gunther asked.

Steven sighed heavily. "In the last few years, the government has been working covertly to silence any opposition, forcing us to go underground. We fear that Mathison has gained so much power that there's very little we can do to stop him at this point from taking complete control of the entire city."

Gunther's complexion suddenly drained of color as the words he had read on the screen back in the lab came flooding into his memory. Braedon and Steven, seeing the change in his countenance, exchanged glances.

"What is it?" Braedon asked in concern. "You had that same look on your face when I first found you in the lab."

His eyes regaining their focus, Gunther looked back and forth between the two men. "It's already too late."

"Why?" Steven said, his voice low. "What did you discover?"

"I didn't mention it when I told you my story because I wasn't sure if I could completely trust you. But after what you just told me. . ." Gunther swallowed hard, then continued, his voice strained. "At the rate things are going, Mathison will be able to control the very minds of the majority of the people of Elysium within less than a year."

"Control their minds?" Braedon asked in astonishment. "But. . .but how?"

"He's going to do it by using the implants from *Pandora's Box!*"

Chapter 12

Conversations

At Gunther's statement, both Steven and Braedon's expressions displayed their shock. Braedon was the first to recover. "The *Pandora's Box* implants? Are you sure it's just those? What about the regular wireless ones? And how could they control people through the implants anyway?"

"As far as the 'how' goes, it appears that Mathison's people helped develop the technology and put within each implant a 'back door' that would allow a central computer to override any other signals. Because the implants are connected directly into the brain, commands from Mathison would be indistinguishable from the person's own thoughts. He'll basically be able to create an army of human robots! Based on what little I read, it doesn't appear that the regular wireless implants would work. The *Pandora's Box* implants are much more complex and connect to more parts of the brain."

"I'm afraid I already know the answer to this question, but. . .why?" Braedon asked.

Gunther's face darkened. "Mathison is preparing for war."

Steven leaned back onto the cushion of the couch, his face showing the weariness of one who had grown tired of fighting. "This is what we had feared," he said, turning toward Braedon. "Only we thought that his ambition was limited to the creation of the Guardians and the Vortex weapon. We never believed he would turn his own citizens into soldiers."

"So you knew he was planning to attack the Jihadists?" Gunther said in surprise. "You knew about the Vortex weapon?"

"Yes," Braedon said. "I suppose we should fill you in on our side of the story." He glanced at Steven to seek his permission. Receiving a slight nod of his head from the older man, Braedon began. "Crimson Liberty has been working to expose the true agenda of Mathison and his cronies for years. I have been working as a soldier and guard for the government for the past eight years. Over time, I became increasingly disturbed by the mandates that were being passed down and the callous way in which some people were treated. Over time, I eventually joined Crimson Liberty.

"Once part of the organization, they felt I could best help the cause by remaining in my post and gathering inside information," Braedon stated. Pausing momentarily, he took a drink of his water, then continued. "Since the inception of the Guardian program, it has become harder and harder to keep my true beliefs hidden. My bosses didn't like the fact that I turned down a chance to become a Cyborg –"

"–that's the slang for a Type I Guardian, right?" Gunther interjected. "Like the one that chased us tonight."

Braedon nodded. "The rest of us 'regular' soldiers came up with names that were easier to work with. All that talk of 'types' just seemed too formal. The Type I technologically enhanced Guardians are called 'Cyborgs', we nicknamed the Type II *genetically* enhanced ones 'Hybrids', and the Type III genetically *and* technologically altered are called 'Titans', from mythology.

"Anyway," Braedon said, reverting back to his original point, "my employers didn't take kindly to my refusal to become a Cyborg, so they demoted me to night guard. I see it now as part of God's plan. By working the night shift, I had more freedom to do some poking around. Eventually it led me to other sympathizers, and we were able to learn about Mathison's true motives. We only recently discovered information about the Vortex weapon and were trying to figure out a way to get our hands on it. You solved that problem for us."

"Glad I could help," Gunther said sarcastically. "I wish I had known about you guys sooner. It would have made things much easier. I almost had a heart attack when you and your partner burst into the room. Speaking of which, how did you find me? What gave me away?"

Braedon took another swig of water before answering. "The security techs noticed that someone was transmitting from an encrypted frequency. It took them a little while, but they finally figured out where the signal was being received. They sent Nick and I to check it out. When we didn't find you the first time, we were told to leave and then double back once the techs were able to shut down the transmission. As you learned first hand, it worked."

Gunther ran his hand through his thinning hair as he processed Braedon's words. "And so, I suppose when you heard me muttering about being able to stabilize the portals, and when you saw that I had downloaded the data and had the Vortex weapon, you figured this would be a once-in-a-lifetime chance. You could use my failed infiltration attempt as a cover-up to escape from the compound."

"Yep. And it worked like a charm," Braedon commented snidely, causing Steven to harrumph loudly. Taking mock offense, Braedon turned toward the dark-skinned man. "Hey, I got us out, didn't I?"

"Yeah," Steven replied. "But you wouldn't have made it very far if Jace hadn't been close enough to come to get you when you called him."

"Called him?" Gunther asked, the lines in his forehead increasing. "But I didn't. . .oh. I see. You have a wireless implant. So that's how you communicated with your Commander. But, aren't those against your religion? I mean, no offense, but I assumed you turned down the chance to become a Guardian because of your religious convictions."

Braedon sighed before answering, as if he had answered this question many times before. "Having a wireless implant isn't specifically against any direct teaching of Christianity. However, I wish I could go back and undo it. I got it a few years prior to my. . .change of heart. Regardless, there's a huge difference between having a small device imbedded into your skin and having scientists and technicians encase your arms and legs with metal and play God with your body. You of all people should know what they do to those men. Didn't you say you worked on the Guardian program?"

Gunther looked embarrassed. "Yes, unfortunately. I was mostly involved in research and development. Actually, it was *because* of my involvement with that program that I started to question the intentions of my superiors. From what I know, it's very fortunate that you didn't agree to join the project. My friend who worked directly on the development of the Guardians confided in me that he sometimes wondered if the. . .Cyborgs, as you call them, had any humanity left. The technological implants make them too much like machines. They rarely speak, and are almost *too* efficient in everything they do. They lack compassion and become disassociated with their families and friends."

Leaning forward so that his elbows rested on his knees, Steven looked first at Braedon, then let his gaze return to Gunther. "The bottom line regarding most technology is that it is neither 'good' nor 'evil'. It's a tool. Technology has a way of bringing out what lies within the human heart. A knife can either cut food or kill a man. A hammer can build a home or destroy a life. Take *Pandora's Box* for example. In the hands of one man, it could be a powerful educational tool used to teach history, or it could help someone overcome their fears by facing them in a virtual world. In the hands of another man, it could be used for perverse pleasures and self-glorifying fantasies, often leading to destroyed personal relationships and the collapse of social functions in the real world."

The sudden image of the woman that Gunther 'helped' while in his *Pandora's Box* session came unbidden to his mind. With it came the memory of his attraction to her and the disturbing thoughts that accompanied it. "I see what you mean," he stated. "Sadly, it appears to me that the average human heart is selfish and lacking in self-control. Otherwise there wouldn't be so many *Box* rehabilitation centers and the government wouldn't need to regulate it."

"Ain't that the truth," Braedon chimed in. "'Public virtue cannot exist in a nation without private virtue, and public virtue is the only foundation of republics.'"

"What was that?" Gunther asked, looking over at Braedon curiously.

"It's just a quote from John Adams that my father drilled into me time and time again," Braedon replied. "He's one of the founding father's of the United States and its second president," he explained for Steven's sake.

"If only more people understood that," Steven commented dryly. "They don't realize that if they don't control themselves, the government has to step in and control them. And when that happens, people lose their freedom. The current culture of Elysium is one where people don't think things through rationally, they just follow their impulses. Many have become so addicted to instant gratification, mindless entertainment and physical stimulation that they've lost the ability to function properly in the real world. Have you seen some of these addicts, Gunther?"

"Not personally, no," he replied.

Steven's expression reflected the pain in his soul. "These poor people have lost their will to live outside of the *Box*. They walk around like mindless zombies. When they first arrive at the rehabilitation centers, we have to actually *feed* them or they wouldn't eat. Even those who aren't addicts have problems thinking clearly. I've talked to so many people that just live in the moment. And it's not just the young people. Many adults have forgotten how to think rationally. Instead of seeing 'through' the eye and *with* the conscience, they see 'with' the eye *devoid* of a conscience. They *think* with their emotions. If something *feels* comfortable, no matter how illogical it may be, they believe it to be true."

"So, is there any hope for Elysium?" Gunther asked sincerely. "How do you propose to change the culture? By imposing your beliefs upon them?"

Braedon seemed somewhat irritated by the scientist's tone. But before he could say anything, Steven cut him off. "First of all, a culture is just the collective beliefs of a group of people. If you can change the *individual* beliefs, then yes, you can make an impact in the culture.

"But I want to make something very clear," Steven said as he leaned toward Gunther. "Christians don't *impose* their beliefs on anyone. We *propose* our beliefs to them. It ultimately comes down to a quest for truth. Unfortunately, because so many people have filled every moment of their lives with entertainment or work, they leave no time to reflect upon the truly important questions – questions about ultimate truth. They've become so easily bored by overstimulation, they don't have the patience or the attention span to think about what matters most in life."

"No offense, but you sound like a preacher," Gunther stated with a sly grin.

"Maybe that's because he is," Braedon said.

"Really?" Gunther said in surprise. "But. . .I mean, he seemed so comfortable with a gun, and Braedon called you a 'Master Sergeant', like you were in the military. Then again, I suppose that just goes along with being a. . .being in the type of organization you're in."

"You mean, being a religious zealot?" Steven clarified.

115

"Well, I didn't mean. . ." Gunther stumbled over his words.

Steven immediately smiled and held up a hand to put Gunther at ease. "No offense taken. Actually, I was a top trainer for the Elysium militia until. . .well, until I decided I'd had enough of their. . .agenda. After that, I decided to spend the rest of my life helping others and doing what I could to further the kingdom of God."

Gunther frowned. "I don't know. Maybe I missed it somewhere, but how does fighting against the government have anything to do with religion? After all, aren't religion and politics two completely separate issues? What do archaic beliefs have to do with the issues facing modern times?"

"My friend, just because beliefs are ancient doesn't mean they aren't true. In fact, there are some truths that are *too important* to be new," Steven explained. "Many of the problems facing us today are due to the philosophy that religion and politics shouldn't intersect. Every decision that a person, and a government, makes is based on the worldview of that person, or institution."

"I take it that when you say 'worldview' you mean how one views the world, right?" Gunther asked.

"Basically," Braedon interjected. "It's a set of underlying beliefs and principles that help form how you view reality."

"But it's deeper than just how you view the world. It's your entire belief system," Steven summarized. "Every decision you make stems from your worldview. Let me give you an example. Do you believe it's wrong to murder someone in cold blood?"

"Of course," Gunther stated emphatically. "Murder is wrong."

"But why? What makes murder wrong?"

Gunther thought for a moment before answering. "I guess I would say because the majority of people agree that it's wrong."

"So, if I convince a majority of people that it's okay to murder someone, would it then become right?" Steven asked.

Becoming increasingly uncomfortable with this line of questioning, Gunther shrugged. "I. . .I guess so."

"Do you really believe that?" Steven asked pointedly. "Let me ask you another question: do you believe that man evolved over millions of years from a single-celled organism?"

"Yes," Gunther stated. "That *is* the prevailing scientific explanation for the origin of life. But how does this relate to a worldview?"

Steven gestured articulately with his hands as he explained. "Just this: you say that murder is wrong, but your worldview contradicts your own beliefs. Based on your own words, I would propose that evolution is your underlying belief system, or your worldview. So when someone asks, is murder wrong, you have to compare that to your belief in evolution. Following logic, if evolution is true, then we live by the rule of survival of the fittest. Therefore, I if I want to murder someone, it shows that I'm better able to survive than the other. Why would that be wrong?"

"But we're more evolved than that," Gunther countered. "We've developed social structures and guiding principles for behavior."

"Okay, but if social structures are just man made, then men can change them whenever they want," Steven replied.

Gunther remained silent for several seconds as he sought a flaw in the man's reasoning. "I understand what you mean now by a worldview. If I follow your logic, you then believe that your Christian worldview – namely that God created every-thing – should form your beliefs about how people should run their lives and how government should work. Is that correct?"

Steven smiled broadly. "Exactly. You see, Gunther, Christianity is more than just a religion. It's a truth claim about what is real. And if that truth is correct, then we should order *every* aspect of our life in line with that truth."

"But what if it isn't real?" Gunther asked.

"That's the very reason why we need to not be so busy and distracted by entertainment," Braedon said. "For if we are, we won't have time to answer these questions."

"Gunther, let me be blunt with you," Steven said, suddenly serious. "We are all wanted men. And if Mathison and his Guardians catch us, we'll likely be killed. So let me ask you: what do you believe is going to happen to you when you die?"

"I'd cease to exist." Although Gunther made this statement casually, his body language showed his conversation partners that his confidence in his pronouncement was less than certain.

"How do you know?" Steven asked.

Thinking back on their discussion, Gunther tried to figure out where this current line of questioning was leading. "Because I believe in evolution, I guess."

"And why do you believe in evolution?"

"Because that's what the scientific majority believes."

"But have you researched it for yourself?" Steven asked.

"Somewhat," Gunther replied. "I've read articles and textbooks about it."

Steven suddenly rose to his feet, stepped over to a cabinet and opened it. A moment later, he withdrew a pistol and pointed it at Gunther. Startled, the scientist tried to move his body out of the line of fire.

"Don't worry, this gun's energy clip is empty," Steven said reassuringly. "See for yourself." He tossed the pistol to Gunther, who caught it nervously. He checked the power readings on the side of the weapon, then handed it back to Steven.

"What was that all about?" Gunther asked, perturbed. "Why did you point an empty gun at me?"

"Would you let me pull the trigger on a gun that was pointed directly at you, even after I told you it was empty?"

"No. I don't want you pointing that thing at me even after I've checked to make sure it's empty," Gunther stated. "You never know."

"Okay, so what you're saying is that you'd want to investigate for yourself before putting your life in danger, and even then you wouldn't want to take the risk" Steven confirmed. "Then why would you do that with your eternal soul? Why wouldn't you do your own research about what awaits you after death? Why do you just trust what others tell you when your *eternal destiny* is at stake?"

Still unnerved by the incident with the gun and with Steven's arguments, Gunther decided he'd had enough for one evening. Standing to his feet, he looked down at the other two men. "Listen, you've both given me plenty to think about, and I want to say thank you once again for saving my life. But as you can imagine, it's been a long day and I need some sleep. If you'd be so kind to point me in the right direction, I think I'll call it a day."

Steven stood and looked at Gunther with genuine concern. "Sure. Your room's upstairs. Follow me." As Steven led the way up the steps, he turned to look at Gunther, who was walking just behind him. "Please, Gunther, understand that saving your life is just the beginning. The stakes are even higher than you're willing to admit. We *do* believe that there's a God and that you have an eternal soul. You can deny the existence of gravity all you want, but if you jump out of a window, you'll still have to face its effects. So we beg you to consider the claims of the Bible. Jesus really was God, and he paid the penalty for our sins. If you ask for forgiveness, He'll wipe away your sins and grant you eternal life with Him in heaven. Don't pass up this chance. None of us knows when we'll take our final breath."

Gunther smiled weakly as Steven stopped just outside the bedroom door. "Thank you for your concern. I'll think about what you've said. Have a good night."

With that, Gunther entered his room and shut the door behind him. Stepping over to the bed, he collapsed onto it and felt the weariness from the day's activities drain out of him. But no matter how much he tried, he found it impossible to sleep. In his mind, he replayed their conversation over and over, trying desperately to escape from the feelings of urgency and uneasiness that Steven's questions evoked. Finally, after more than an hour, exhaustion overwhelmed him and he drifted off into a shallow, restless sleep.

Chapter 13

The Visitor

Gunther was awakened by the muffled sounds of voices and someone moving around outside the bedroom door. For a moment, his sleep-addled brain didn't recognize his surroundings, and panic swept over him, causing him to sit up abruptly in the bed. When the memory of the previous evening's activities finally surfaced, it brought with it another wave of panic. *Who's outside the door? Did they find us? Where are Braedon and Steven? Slow down, Gunther you ol' fool. Don't jump to conclusions. If it was the police, I doubt they'd be talking at all.* Dragging his weary body out of bed, he stepped carefully over to the door and placed his ear against it to listen.

His breathing eased as he recognized the voices of his companions. Straining to hear, he tried to make out what was being said, his fear having now turned to curiosity. However, before he could comprehend anything, a sudden knock on his door startled him. Backing away from it so that the others wouldn't think he was spying on them, he waited a moment, then responded. "Yes?"

"Sorry to wake you, but it's almost six o'clock," Steven's muffled voice said from the other side of the door. "We need to decide what to do next, and we should probably get moving before the Globe reaches full light output."

"Alright. I'll be out in a moment," Gunther replied. After taking a minute to straighten his clothes and run his fingers through his thinning gray hair, Gunther opened the door and joined the others in the downstairs living room where they had met the night before.

"Good morning," Gunther said sluggishly as he still fought to awaken his body. As he sat on the couch next to Braedon, he massaged his face and eyes with his hands. "Do you guys happen to have any coffee?" he murmured.

"Sure, just give me a moment," Steven said. "Cream or sugar?"

"No thanks. Black will be just fine."

Steven headed upstairs and returned a moment later with a cup of steaming coffee, which Gunther gratefully accepted. Steven then returned to the wooden chair that faced the couch and sat down. "Braedon and I think it would be best if we got an early start this morning. We don't want to stay in one place for too long. With that in mind, we also need to decide what our next step should be. You indicated that you could stabilize the portals. How? What do you need to make that happen?"

Gunther hesitated a moment before answering. "When I broke into the compound, I was hoping to find the prototype of the Portal Stabilizer, but I didn't. So, Plan B was to download the research notes so that I could build another one. Which, come to think of it, you should still have the storage drive in your pocket." Gunther said, addressing Braedon. "May I. . .may I have it back?"

"Sure," he replied as he withdrew the mini storage drive from his shirt pocket. Based on the casualness of his response, Gunther guessed that the information contained within its memory had already been copied.

Gunther took the offered device from Braedon, examined it quickly for damage, then tucked it into his pants' pocket as he continued speaking. "The information on this drive represents years of work. With it, I should be able to reconstruct another prototype within. . .I don't know, six months, if I can get the materials and tools I need."

"Six months?" Braedon echoed. Looking over at Steven, he stared at him intently. "It looks like you were right. We can't stay here that long. We'll have to find another location." Turning back to Gunther, he asked, "And what about materials? I'm assuming we're going to have to get some sophisticated stuff for you to build that thing."

Steven cut in, "We can worry about materials later. First things first. We can't stay here in Elysium. We've got enough connections in the rest of Tartarus, so we should be able to get what we need. We'll just have to pray that Mathison doesn't attack Bab al-Jihad before we can get the prototype built. If he does, it'll likely drag all of Tartarus into the conflict, making it nearly impossible for us to get the materials."

"There is another option," Gunther said hesitantly. "It seems that the Vortex weapon was designed from the Stabilizer's blueprints. It's possible that I could modify it so that it'll work just like the Stabilizer. Unfortunately, I haven't had time to look over the data I downloaded to even determine if that's feasible."

"Do you know what the Vortex does?" Braedon asked.

"No. Do you?"

Braedon shook his head. "We only know that Mathison believes it will give his army a huge edge over the Jihadists. I guess we'll have to count on you to take a look at that data to find out the answer."

"We need to buy ourselves some more time," Steven stated. "So the question is: where do we go?"

"What about Cameron's group?" Braedon replied. "He's got enough extra space, and since he's only a few miles from New China, we would be able to get the parts we need easily enough."

Steven considered the idea, then discarded it. "It's too far away. We need something closer."

The two men quickly became so engrossed in their private conversation that they seemed to completely ignore Gunther. Finally, after several minutes of listening to the men debate the pros and cons of each Crimson Liberty location, he interrupted them by clearing his throat loudly.

"What about Dehali," Gunther said. "I've got a friend there who can help me. He was the one I told you about who broke into the system."

Steven's brow furrowed as he considered the suggestion. "We do know a couple of people in Dehali who are sympathetic to our cause, but their facilities are not nearly as secure as some of our other locations."

"But I need him," Gunther reiterated. "With his help, I could probably complete the portal device in half the time. Together I'm sure that we could—"

A loud crash that came from somewhere outside the house cut off the remainder of Gunther's sentence. The three men froze where they sat. When a second scuffling sound and thud were heard, Steven and Braedon leapt from their seats and headed cautiously up the stairs as they drew laser pistols from their concealed holsters.

Left alone, Gunther scanned the room for signs of the bag that contained the Vortex weapon. After half a minute of searching, he found it tucked underneath a chair in the corner. As he prepared to grab it, he heard steps on the stairs behind him. Spinning around, he was relieved to see Braedon and Steven returning, the tension gone from their faces.

"What was it? What's goin' on?" Gunther asked.

Steven appeared relaxed but pensive as he stepped off the last of the stairs. "We've got an unexpected visitor."

"A visitor?" Gunther stated, a frown creasing his face. "What kind of visitor? Are we in any danger?"

Braedon held up a reassuring hand. "No. It's nothing to be worried about. It's just that. . .we're not in the nicest part

of the city, so from time to time, we get. . .stragglers, . . .vaga-
bonds. . .or. . .or addicts that show up on our doorstep."

"Actually, it's one of the reasons Crimson Liberty owns
this house," Steven explained. "You see, Gunther, we're much
more than just an organization dedicated to speaking out
against tyranny. As we mentioned last night, one of our pri-
mary objectives is to fight for the sanctity of life – that means
all life. If we didn't try to help people, our rhetoric would be
hollow and meaningless."

"So. . .what are you saying?" Gunther asked. "Are you sug-
gesting that there's some drug addict at the door and you want
to let him in and help him? I don't think that's a good idea.
He might be. . .crazy or something. He might rob us, or. . .or
worse."

Braedon shook his head. "I don't think so. The way he's
been acting and carrying on, it looks like he's suffering from
the after-affects of a night of marathon *Box* sessions."

"Don't worry, Gunther," Steven reassured him. "We've
helped many people like this man before. First, we'll wait to see
if he snaps out of it and heads home by himself. If he doesn't,
we'll bring him in, give him a little something to eat with some
coffee, and see if that works. If not, then we'd normally take
him to a rehabilitation center. However, under the present circumstances, we'll just have to alert some of the other members
of Crimson Liberty and have them come over to take care of
him."

"I'm not sure this is a good idea," Braedon said, his voice
low as he approached his dark-skinned mentor to speak pri-
vately. "We've got enough to worry about right now. I think
God would excuse us for not helping a man just this once."

"Braedon, I'm not going to leave him vulnerable to being
robbed or beaten just because I'm busy," Steven countered, the
volume of his voice loud enough so that Gunther would be
included in the conversation. "Besides, we need to eat and get
ready to leave anyway. This man isn't going to slow us down."

"I still think this is a mistake," Braedon stated.

"You know my philosophy," Steven said with a lighthearted smile. "If you're going to err, err on the side of compassion. If you get burned for your generosity, then rest assured that your reward in heaven will be even greater. My faith tells me that if we somehow get caught because we helped a lost soul, God will take care of us. Trust Him with the outcome."

Having finished, Steven headed up the stairs to check on their visitor. Braedon stood silent for a moment, lost in his thoughts. Gunther walked up to stand next to him, a frown creasing his brow. "He is *definitely* a preacher. If it's any consolation, I agree with you. We've got more important things to do besides baby-sit some low-life. And what if this one addict causes us to fail in our plans and costs the lives of millions? Has Steven thought of that?"

Braedon shook his head in disagreement. "No. He's right. A single human life, made in the image of God, is more important than anything. Jesus said that the good shepherd would leave the ninety-nine to help the one lost sheep. If we only help others when it's convenient, then we undermine everything that we stand for."

"Well, even if you guys aren't 'terrorists', you *are* religious zealots," Gunther said, his tone carrying a hint of derision.

Although a sharp reply sprang immediately into his mind, Braedon decided to let the comment slide. Turning, he headed up the stairs with Gunther following behind.

When they arrived at the top of the steps, they could see that the light from the Globe was now close to seventy-five percent. Since Gunther arrived in the middle of the night, he took a few moments to examine his surroundings. The house was of average size and seemed to consist of a single floor, plus the finished basement. The kitchen was rather small, but the dining area next to it made it seem larger. In the front of the house, Gunther could see the morning light streaming in through the closed curtains, illuminating the plain, tan furniture that had clearly seen better days. Altogether the house was not the finest place he had ever stayed in, it was warm and inviting.

Gunther's attention was drawn back to Steven as he opened the front door of the house, which led into the living room. He stepped outside, then returned a moment later supporting a young man who clearly seemed out of touch with reality. The visitor looked to be in his mid-twenties, and was a couple of inches shorter than Steven. His medium-length, dark, wavy hair was unkempt, his strong jaw sported a five o'clock shadow with matching mustache, and his second-hand clothes were wrinkled and disheveled. Had he been better dressed, his hair combed and his face clean-shaven, he would have been quite handsome. However, in his current state, Gunther felt nothing but disgust toward the man.

Once they were inside, Braedon closed the door and reached out to help Steven. However, the man suddenly pulled away from him and fell sideways onto the coffee table that rested in front of the couch. Looking up at the three men from atop the table, the visitor started waving his left hand at them as if trying to shoo them away.

"No. . .no that's not right," the man murmured. "Computer, return to the main menu. Computer. . .COMPUTER!"

Steven stepped forward and helped the man onto the nearby couch. "Can you hear me? Sir, what's your name?"

The man studied Steven for a moment, a confused look on his face. "Wait a second. . .this isn't the way the *Intrepid* looks. Computer. . .end program. Return to the main menu."

"Sir, what is your name?" Steven tried again. "Can you hear me?"

"Be careful how you address me, soldier," the man replied. "Don't you know who I am?"

"No, sir," Steven said. "Who are you?"

"I'm General Cornelius. I'm in charge of the fleet. Now, release me and tell me what you've done with the Ambassador. I need to speak to him immediately!"

"Pardon me, General Cornelius," Steven replied. "We've been sent to see to your needs. Just lay down here on the couch and let me bring you something to eat."

Gunther was amazed at Steven's patience. Had he been in his shoes, he would have taken extreme pleasure in throwing the man out into the street by his ear, not catering to him. He couldn't understand why Steven was wasting his time. Deciding he'd had enough, Gunther stepped back into the kitchen to help Braedon, who had begun cooking some eggs and toast. Within a couple of minutes, Steven had the man settled onto the couch and came into the kitchen to grab a plate of food for their 'guest'.

After handing it to him and trying to get him to eat, Steven returned to the dining room and sat at the table with the others. "He's resting now. Maybe he'll be better off when he wakes up. As soon as we're finished eating, I'm going to contact the others and have one of them help him."

"At least you tried," Braedon commented.

"Yeah," Steven said distractedly as he took a bite of food. "The funny thing is. . .he looks familiar to me. I think I may have seen him bef–"

The clicking of the side door lock as it popped open was all the warning the three men were given.

Three people burst into the house, two from the side door that led into the kitchen and one from the front door. The first to enter was a huge, burly man with long, blond hair that hung down just past his shoulders. He rushed into the kitchen area and grabbed Steven, who was closest to the door, and lifted him out of his chair. Following instantly behind the man was a thin woman of Asian descent.

Reacting to the sudden attack, Braedon pushed himself back from the table and drew his pistol. However, before he could point it at a target, the woman kicked out with her leg and sent the weapon flying from his grasp. Now weaponless, Braedon struck out at the woman with a series of punches, which were limited by the cramped space of the dining room. His opponent smiled broadly as she easily blocked each attack. Stunned by her speed and grace, Braedon realized that he was clearly outmatched. After a few more moments of toying with him, the woman executed a flurry of attacks with amazing precision, sending Braedon crashing to the floor in pain.

Meanwhile, the third person that had entered through the front door rushed in and placed a gun against Gunther's temple as he attempted to escape from the melee in the dining room.

"Don't move, any of you," the third man said in a commanding voice.

Staring up slowly at him, Gunther was surprised to see that neither this man, nor the other two were dressed in anything that resembled military or police uniforms. Instead, they were dressed in plain street clothes. Furthermore, Gunther was surprised to note that the man holding the gun was Arabic.

With their captives under control, the large man holding Steven dropped him unceremoniously into one of the kitchen chairs and stood alert behind him. As Steven recovered from the chokehold, he looked up at the Arabic man and their eyes locked. The surprise on both of their faces made it instantly obvious to everyone in the room that the two knew each other.

"Well, well, well," the man said, his voice filled with amusement. "This is quite an unexpected surprise. It's so nice to see you again, 'Master'!"

Chapter 14

Raptor

S ilence settled over the room as the two men stared at each other. After several moments, Steven spoke. "It's good to see you too, Rahib. And I honestly mean that, despite the circumstances."

The man's face hardened almost imperceptibly, causing a muscle in his cheek to twitch. "I don't go by that name anymore. Call me Raptor."

Although the man had an Arabic accent, and the dark skin and features common to that culture, his hair was trimmed in a style more common to modern Elysium. He looked to be about thirty years old, and, like his two accomplices, he was in excellent physical shape. His silky black dress shirt and his pencil-thin mustache and goatee made his handsome face all the more striking. To Gunther's mind, the man's overall appearance seemed more suited for a business office.

"A new name won't change your present. . .or your past," Steven countered.

Ignoring the comment, the man turned to look at Gunther. "You can go ahead and sit back down at the table."

As Gunther nervously obeyed his order, Raptor turned to look at the Asian woman. "Jade, help that one into his chair. There's no reason why we can't be more civilized." Immediately,

she stooped over and helped her pain-wracked, former opponent into his chair. Braedon groaned and leaned heavily on the
table as he regained consciousness.

"Charon, make sure the area's secure," Raptor said. As the
big man headed past the group and into the living room, he
nearly collided with another man who was just stepping into
the kitchen.

"Whoa! You almost ran me over! Watch out for us little
folk, huh?"

Gunther felt his heart sink into his stomach as he recognized the newcomer.

"Move it or lose it," Charon said as he pushed past the
man. "And go comb your hair. You look like a freak!"

The 'visitor' smiled as he moved into the kitchen and leaned
up against the wall. "Thank you, gentlemen, for the breakfast.
The eggs were particularly delicious."

Steven frowned and seemed to be fighting against his own
emotions as he studied the man. "So it *was* an act after all," he
stated in disgust. "How noble of you to use a man's compassion against him."

"Hey, it's nothing personal," the man countered. "It just
seemed like the most efficient way to gain entry. We'd heard
that you Crimson Liberty types were a bit soft when it comes
to lowlifes, so we thought we'd see if it was true. Actually, you
helped me win a little wager with Jade. She didn't think I'd even
succeed in getting inside, much less be able to get the remote
to figure out the door lock combination in time."

"Shut up, Traverse," the Asian woman said snidely, although
her slight grin softened her harsh words.

"Traverse?" Steven echoed. His expression suddenly
changed as his mind put the pieces together. "Xavier Traverse,
the former actor turned con artist. I thought you looked
familiar."

"Former?" he replied with a raised eyebrow, clearly
affronted. "After such a successful performance?"

Ignoring the eccentric man, Steven turned his attention back to the leader of the group. "So, Rahib," he began, deliberately refusing to use the man's code name, "what misfortune have you encountered that you've been forced to surround yourself with such. . .colorful characters?"

Smiling, the Arabic man leaned toward Steven. "I could ask you the same question. In addition, I could add, 'What would cause a disgraced ex-soldier to break into a government compound and steal data and a weapon? Tell me, 'preacher', isn't it against your religion to steal?"

Steven didn't back down. "If you want to talk about religion, I'm all for that. But somehow, I don't think that you really want to hear my answer. How did you know about the weapon, and what's in this for you? I can guarantee you that Crimson Liberty would be willing to make you a counter offer."

Raptor leaned back as he began running his fingers across the surface of the gun. "Let's just say that Xavier here happened to be at the right place at the right time. Your little spat with the Cyborg was quite spectacular, from what I hear. And although the invisibility cloaks are quite effective against the casual observer, . . .well, Xavier *isn't* a casual observer."

"What can I say?" Xavier shrugged. "I'm gifted."

"As for the purpose of your little duel, that wasn't hard to piece together if you know how to read between the lines of the unofficial government transmissions," Raptor continued. "Actually, our meeting is quite fortuitous. We've recently had a. . .falling out with a. . .powerful individual. The bounty we'll receive from turning you in should go a long way in making amends. Your two friends here have become quite famous, in case you haven't heard. Your pictures have been transmitted to all implant customers and to all personal hand-held devices. Everyone in Elysium knows what you look like by now."

"Raptor," Steven began, hoping that the use of his preferred name would help to increase the impact of his words, "there's more at stake here than you know. Crimson Liberty may not be able to match the cash the government could give, but we can make up for it in other ways."

Raptor smiled. "I doubt it. You're not exactly the most popular or powerful group around."

This time, it was Steven who leaned forward, causing Jade to tense in case he chose to move any further. "Listen. I don't know what you've been told about me, but I need you to hear me out. Can we. . .can I talk to you alone?"

The Arabic man's eyes narrowed as he considered the request. "Fine. Jade, Xavier, watch these two."

"Sure thing," Xavier said cheerfully. "Then again, this one doesn't look like he's going to be much trouble anytime soon," he commented as he sat down near Braedon. "What did you do to him, Jade?"

Her reply faded into the background as Steven and Raptor headed down the stairs. When they reached the bottom, Raptor paused, the gun still pointed at Steven's back. "Do I have your word that you won't try to escape during our little 'chat'?"

"Yes, you can trust me," Steven said.

"Huh. Trust. That's interesting, coming from a man who lied to his family, and all those who looked up to him," Raptor said with venom in his voice.

Steven continued to look straight at the younger man, his face impassive. "I know that's what you've heard, but it isn't true."

"Oh really? Then please, enlighten me," Raptor said sarcastically.

Sitting down on the couch, Steven closed his eyes a moment before speaking. "Look, Rah. . .Raptor. It seems that you've already made up your mind about me, and I don't know if anything I can tell you will change that. However, I promise you by everything that I hold dear in this world that what I'm about to tell you is absolutely true."

Raptor sat opposite Steven and began playing with his goatee, his expression hard. Steven looked calmly at his companion as he began speaking. "I'm sure by now you of all people have seen the corruption that is at the core of the Mathison administration. He and his people think that they're above the law – that what they're doing is creating a more perfect world. And they'll stop at nothing to achieve their goals. Well, I got in the way."

"Of course you did."

"As you probably know, about seven years ago I resigned from the military and started speaking out against the laws that were being passed by Mathison," Steven continued. "I guess you could say I made myself an easy target. Mathison and his men knew that, as a former military trainer, I had too much loyalty among the other soldiers. So, they decided that the only way to silence me was to discredit my character."

"They framed you?" Raptor asked, the tone of his voice skeptical, yet uncertain.

Steven nodded. "They planted fake texts and e-mails onto my phone and personal computer, making it look like I'd been having an affair with another woman. They got a woman to make up detailed stories about me. Then, to make things worse, they took money out of my account and made it look like I stole from my wife, leaving her penniless. The media had a field day. They blasted me as a liar, a thief, and a home-wrecker. My wife left me, and my children won't speak to me even to this day. I lost everything overnight, all because I chose to speak out."

Raptor considered his words for a moment. "You expect me to believe that a man with your experience and intelligence so easily fell into such a foolish trap? Am I to believe that you didn't at least prepare your own family for what could come if you spoke out? C'mon. Don't insult my intelligence. Do you take me for a fool?"

"Of course not," Steven retaliated, his voice rising slightly in agitation. "But you know as well as I do how proficient Mathison is at twisting the truth. Although I warned my family,

Mathison's people managed to make it look like I knew the truth was going to come out and I was trying to cover my tracks. They certainly did their homework. They dug up some things from my wife's pain-filled past and played off of her innate fears. They did a masterful job of manipulating events."

Raptor narrowed his eyes at his former master, and for a heartbeat, Steven thought that his chance of convincing the man of his innocence had been lost. Then, to his relief, Raptor relaxed his stance slightly. "Five years ago I don't think I would've believed you no matter what excuse you came up with," he said. "But you're right. Since then, I've seen firsthand what Mathison is capable of."

Grateful that hope still remained, Steven pressed the point. "Which is why it's so urgent that you listen to me now," he said. "I don't know what you've been doing since that night you left ten years ago. All I know is that during the six years that you were under my teaching, I could see so much potential in you. You are intelligent, a quick thinker, and you have a sharp mind. But, you also carried a heavy burden of pain buried deep inside. Just when I felt you start to trust me and open up, you. . .left."

"Well, what did you expect me to do after I'd just killed a man for messing with my girl? Stick around for tea?" Raptor remarked snidely.

"I'm not here to judge you for what you did. But you can't let your past determine your future."

"Where are you going with this?" Raptor asked, his impatience growing.

"I need your help," Steven implored. "This whole thing with the Vortex weapon is bigger than you. . .it's bigger than all of us! It's definitely bigger than any payoff you might receive for turning us in. I'm not exaggerating when I say that every person in Tartarus is going to be affected one way or another. And as things stand right now, you'll be the one to determine the course of events."

"C'mon, Steven, you don't have to sound so dramatic," Raptor replied. "What's so important about this weapon anyway?"

"The Vortex is just a part of it," Steven explained. "Mathison knows that the leaders of Bab al-Jihad are gathering their strength to attack, so he's begun building an army. He believes that the Guardians – and, from what we understand, the Vortex – will give him an additional edge. But Mathison's also planning on using the *Pandora's Box* implants to control the minds of the citizens of Elysium! He's going to turn everyone in the city that has the implants into soldiers!"

Raptor was silent for several seconds as he digested the news. "I knew he was crazy, but even *I* didn't expect this," he said at last. With his right hand, he reached up to touch the spot where is own implant was housed. His face filled with disgust as he swore. "That could be a problem, considering that I, and everyone I know, has that blasted implant! I'm *not* going to just sit around and allow myself to become someone's puppet. I want to see that data you retrieved."

"Absolutely," Steven said. While he was empathetic with Raptor's predicament, he was also relieved that it was serving the purpose of winning him over to his side.

"Actually, your story makes sense of some other facts," Raptor said. "Mathison has had several of the criminal bosses on his payroll doing odd jobs for the past couple of years. I've even worked for him a couple of times. But none of us really understood what he was trying to accomplish. We just did our jobs and didn't ask questions, which is exactly why he hired us.

"Now I see," Raptor continued. "Sometimes he sent us after information, other times, it was technology or materials, and yet other times, it was people - scientists, mostly. All of which he was using to develop the *Pandora's Box* implants and the Vortex weapon."

"But there's even more to it than that," Steven said. "The elderly gentleman upstairs is a particle physicist who used to work for the government. It was his research that Mathison used to make the Vortex. But that wasn't its original purpose. It was designed to stabilize the portals. With the data he stole from the compound last night, Gunther believes he can modify the Vortex weapon so it will make the portals go both directions! We can leave Tartarus and return to Earth!"

Raptor's skepticism was blatant. "They've been trying to find a way back for over two hundred years. Now you're telling me that they might have succeeded?"

"You don't have to take *my* word for it. Look at the data yourself."

"I fully intend to," Raptor replied.

"Do you see now why we need your help?" Steven asked. "You *can't* turn us in to the government. If you do, then Mathison will win, you and your friends will become living robots for an egomaniac, and no one will ever know that the way back to Earth was ever discovered. But if you help us, we can stop Mathison by opening the portals. And, once we're on Earth, it's a chance for everyone to have a new beginning – a clean slate."

Raptor stood, walked over to a bookshelf and began staring blankly at its contents as he considered Steven's words. "A clean slate, huh?" he said softly. "Even being on Earth won't wipe away the past. It'll always remain. No. Earth is a chance for a new life, not a clean slate."

Steven rose and moved behind Raptor. Placing a hand on his shoulder, he said, "Rahib, I never did find out what caused you to leave home when you were so young, and, honestly, I don't need to know. But *God* knows. If you would only–"

Raptor spun around and knocked Steven's hand from his shoulder. "Don't talk to me about your *God!*" he spat. "He's part of the problem!"

Shocked by his companion's vehemence, Steven took a step back. "I. . .I didn't mean to offend you. But if you tell me what happened, maybe I could. . ."

"No," Raptor said, more calmly. "Getting into a religious discussion with you is the *last* thing I want to do."

"That may be true, but figuring out what you believe is the *most* important topic a person could discuss," Steven replied. "Each religion makes a truth claim that needs to be examined, like a jury trying to decide a court case. You have to examine the evidence, listen to the witnesses and see which one has the strongest argument."

"I don't have time for that," Raptor stated. "I've got more important things to do with my life."

Steven took a step toward Raptor, his arms gesturing as he spoke. "But don't you see, the question of what'll happen to you when you die needs to be answered *now!* None of us is guaranteed another breath. You might die. . ."

A blank look came over Steven's face and his eyes changed their focus, as if they were seeing into another reality. Noting the change on his former mentor's face, Raptor frowned. "Hey, are you alright?"

Steven blinked several times as tears filled his eyes. He stumbled backward as if dizzy and fell to the floor in front of the couch, his right side propped up against it. "Dear God, no. . .please, let there be some other way. . ."

Bending down, Raptor grabbed the other man by his shoulders and stared into his eyes. "Steven, look at me. What's wrong?"

Raptor's former mentor stared up at him, a haunted look on his face. "I. . .you won't. . ." His voice faltered as he struggled with his emotions. Turning away, he spoke softly. "Lord, he. . .he won't understand."

Realizing that Steven was talking to his invisible God, Raptor pulled away in disgust. He never understood how someone so intelligent could be so blinded by religion. Turning to leave, he stopped in his tracks as Steven began to speak, his voice troubled and filled with anguish. "This is what the Lord says:

You have cursed my name for many years,
And have despised those who speak my word.
Why? Because one you loved chose truth instead of lies,
Life, instead of darkness.

Now, the lives of thousands rest in your hands,
Tens of thousands will live or perish by your choices
Your fate is bound to theirs.
The days of your life are now numbered.

Only by opening the door to a new life
Will your own be saved
You must seek out truth,
For only the truth will set you free.

The days of your life are now numbered,
They will be thirty and one!"

"What. . .what was that all about?" Raptor stated, his voice faltering slightly. "Are you trying to scare me or something? Do you think some cryptic message supposedly from 'God' is going to make me want to help you? Well, it won't work." From the expression on his face, Steven could tell that he was unnerved, despite his bravado.

Steven returned his gaze. "No, Rahib. This is not some game. I've only heard the Lord speak *this* clearly to me one other time in my life. This isn't something I'd make up. Besides, I don't even know the meaning of half of it. As I said before, I don't know your past. If what I said makes sense to you, then you'll know that what I've spoken is from God."

Based on the expressions that flitted across Raptor's face, Steven could tell that his mind was waging a vicious internal war. After several seconds of fierce conflict, rage emerged as the victor. Swearing violently, Raptor lunged forward with both hands and grabbed Steven by the front of his shirt. "You religious types are all the same. Trying to use 'God' to manipulate and control people. Well guess what? I'm my own man! You hear me? I won't be controlled by anyone! Especially not some lying, home-wrecking hypocrite! So you can take your. . .contrived little prophecy and shove it back down your throat. I will *not* be intimidated! I AM MY OWN MAN!"

Calmly enduring the tirade, Steven merely looked at Raptor with a mixture of pity and sadness. "Raptor," Steven said, using his code name so as not to enrage him further, "I wish that God would use someone else to speak to you. Since you've refused to accept His words, He will give you two signs."

Raptor narrowed his eyes, trying to decide if he was going to strike Steven, or hear him out. "I'm done with this conversation," he said at last as he pushed Steven away from him. Turning his back on his former master, he began heading toward the steps. However, as his foot touched the bottom step, Steven's words caused him to stop in his tracks.

"The first sign has already been given to you in the form of a dream," Steven said, his voice low and somber. "In it, you are walking through dark caverns being chased by an unknown creature. But in one particular cave, there is. . .a sword."

To Steven's own ears the words sounded foolish. But as Raptor slowly turned to face him, he could see that for the first time, real fear had gripped the other man. Taking a deep breath, Steven continued speaking. "This dream has plagued you now for some time, and will continue to do so as a reminder of the truth until the end of your days.

"The second sign is yet to come. Before this day is finished, the Lord of Hosts will demonstrate His power to you by preserving your life." As Steven finished, Raptor stepped closer to him, his fear turning to confusion.

"How. . .how did you know about my dreams? Only one other knows about them," Raptor said. Suddenly, his expression transformed once more into hatred. "Oh, I get it now. You've somehow figured out how Mathison is going to use the

Box implants to put dreams in my head. Or, just maybe, you're working *for* Mathison! Maybe this is all some kind of elaborate plan concocted by those government wackos."

Steven's unbelief spilled over from his face into his voice, coloring his words. "How can you believe that? I don't. . .I don't know anything about your past! I don't even know what the beginning of the prophecy is referring to!"

"But others do," Raptor countered. "I don't know how you dug up that information, but it's really a sick joke."

"Listen, Rahi–Raptor," Steven said determinedly. "Believe what you want for now. But once the second sign appears, you will have to face the truth. God has spoken to you, and I implore you to listen to Him. You only have thirty-one days left to live! You can no longer run from the hard questions about life and what will happen when you die. You need to find answers before it's too late! And, although the wording of the prophecy can be interpreted in more than one way, it seems that the only chance you have of saving yourself is to open the 'doorway to a new life'. Don't you see? You have to open the portal back to Earth!"

Hardening his resolve, Raptor shook his head. "There is no God. There is no cosmic, all-powerful being that created everything. No one knows what's going to happen when we die. There's *no way* anyone can know, since no one comes back from the grave to tell the rest of us. It's a one-way, mysterious trip that everyone faces alone. And until I have to go down that road, I'm going to get as much pleasure out of this world as I can. I'm not going to live my life bound by some archaic laws and rules made up by power hungry men."

"But there *is* a way to know!" Steven argued. "There *are* ways to know for sure. Look," he said as he removed a small device from his pocket, "I was once like you. I didn't think there was any way a person could know for sure what lies beyond death's door." Removing a small memory chip from the side of the device, he handed it to Raptor. "I did a lot of reading and research. This is my personal journal, where I summarized my findings and copied down some key quotes. Over the past several years, I've organized them so that they would make the most sense. I think you'll get more out of reading this than by me trying to explain everything. Please, read it and seriously consider—"

"You're wasting your time," Raptor snarled, holding out the memory chip for Steven to take. "I'm not interested. Even *if* you could convince me there's a God, he's not the kind of God I want to serve. He's impotent and cruel, and a poor manager of affairs here in Tartarus, and from what I hear, on Earth as well. I will *not* bow my knee to him, or any other god."

If Raptor had anything more to say on the matter, it was cut off by the sound of heavy footsteps on the stairs. Turning toward the steps, Raptor and Steven saw the large form of Charon appear a moment later.

"Sorry to interrupt, but I thought you'd want to know that we've detected quite a bit of activity coming from the police transmissions," he said, a hint of urgency in his voice. "It appears their doing a sweep of the city, starting at the Research and Records compound and working their way out. At that rate, they'll be in this area in a few hours. It may be better if we move this little party of ours to one of our own bases on the outskirts of the city."

Raptor threw one last glance in Steven's direction, then nodded to Charon. "Fine. Pull the hovervan next to the house, then get these three into the back. Xavier and I will follow in the truck. And make sure that you put an implant inhibitor on the troublemaker. We don't want him calling for help."

Without hesitation, Charon followed orders. Stepping past Raptor, he grabbed Steven by the arm and practically shoved him toward the stairs, his disdain for the preacher clearly evident. Raptor watched until the two men had reached the top of the stairs. Once they were out of sight, he looked down at the small memory chip that he still held in his hand. Part of him wanted to smash it, the other part was curious about what arguments could persuade a man such as Steven to become such a radical extremist. His curiosity gaining the upper hand, he pocketed the item and headed up the stairs.

Chapter 15

Truth

*R*aptor sat in the passenger seat of the electric, wheeled pickup truck as Xavier drove. Behind them, the hovervan containing Jade, Charon and their three captives followed. Once the group had turned onto the main road leading to their base, Raptor took out the mini storage drive that he had taken from Gunther and plugged it into his portable holoscreen. The instant he touched the 'on' button, the device projected a holographic screen the size of a standard sheet of paper that hovered three inches in front of the palm-sized unit. In less than ten seconds, the entire contents of the drive had been loaded into the reader. Less than a minute after that, the information had been transferred wirelessly into Raptor's own digital storage device implanted in his skull. He repeated the process for Steven's journal, and, after a few more moments, put the storage devices back into his pants pocket. Returning his attention back to the holoscreen, he began perusing the files that Gunther had stolen from the government computer.

"What's all that stuff?" Xavier asked as he drove.

"Some data that our guests took from the government," he said absentmindedly, his attention still fixed on the screen. "I'll fill you guys in when we get back to the shop." Having worked with his current partner long enough, Xavier recognized the cue that he shouldn't ask any more questions and left Raptor alone to read.

For the next twenty minutes, Raptor scanned through the various files in order to confirm what he had been told. After reading all of the classified memos, he flipped through some of the various diagrams and charts. Satisfied that Steven and the others had been telling the truth, and that he had a pretty good idea of what the rest of the documents contained, he exited out of the files.

However, as he was about to turn off the device, he remembered Steven's journal. Curiosity getting the better of him, he opened up the first entry and began to read.

To my sons: Steven, Jr. and Seth

I know that you've heard many terrible things about me and are ashamed to be called my sons. My prayer is that you will read this journal and come to know that Christianity is true. Even more than that, I pray that you will ACT upon that truth and accept the forgiveness that only Jesus can provide. Secondly, my hope is that after reading my journal, you will come to realize that I would NEVER do the things which the government and media have claimed. For if I had, it would undermine EVERYTHING that I stand for. It would contradict everything that I believe.

I will try to keep these notes as easy to understand as possible, and offer as many examples as I can. I love you both.

Your father

Truth

Before I get into what it is that I believe, I need to lay a foundation and define a few terms. For starters, have you ever wondered what truth really is? Is truth absolute (true for all people, at all times, in all places) or is it relative (does it change based on circumstances)? In other words, does truth change from culture to culture? Is truth the same for those born two thousand years ago as it is for those born today?

According to the dictionary, truth is defined as: *conformity with fact or reality*. By its very definition, truth is *'that which is real'*.

So, can truth change with circumstances? Can something be true for one person, but not for another?

There is something called the *Law of Non-Contradiction*. Don't let the name confuse you. It simply means that something can't EXIST and NOT EXIST at the same time (of course, this assumes that it is equal in all ways). To put it another way, truth can't contradict itself.

Example: I cannot BE in Elysium and NOT BE in Elysium at the same time in the same way, or I cannot BE a man and NOT BE a man simultaneously.

Although this seems like a stupid point to make, in reality, this law is crucial in order to know anything. Without it, we couldn't reason or make any positive claim about anything in life or in the universe. Without this law, science itself wouldn't exist.

Now, let's apply this to the idea of truth. Something can't be true (real) for one person and not true for another. If that were the case, then it wouldn't be real! Remember, truth, by definition, is what is REAL. But many people deny that absolute truth even exists. I've heard people say before that there are no absolutes. But that statement contradicts itself! Do you see the logical fallacy? The statement that there "are no absolutes" IS an absolute statement itself! Therefore, it is self-refuting.

Another thing I've heard often is that, "All truth is relative. What's true for you may not be true for me." But, when you think about it, what they're really saying is, "That MAKES SENSE to you and SEEMS RIGHT to you, but not to me." They aren't really using the term "truth" to mean "what is real."

Okay, so what's the point to all of this mental gymnastics? Well, keeping in mind everything I've said so far, I want to try to answer another question and define another term. What is religion? Religion, in a nutshell, is a truth claim. It's a set of statements that seeks to define reality. In other words, it's a search for truth! Now, since there are many different religions, there are many different truth claims. Obviously, in places where *the religions contradict one another, they both cannot be true (Law of Non-Contradiction).*

Example: Religion is like a scientific hypothesis. Scientists develop a hypothesis to explain why chemicals react certain ways under certain conditions, then they design experiments to test whether their ideas match reality. In the same way, religions offer explanations for why and how the universe exists, how it functions, and how to fix it. When people follow a certain religion, they are basically saying that they believe that Religion A better explains reality than Religion B. Science seeks to explain the reality of the natural, and religion seeks to explain the reality of the supernatural.

This means that in each area of doctrine (set of beliefs) for each religion, we need to question how that doctrine matches reality. After all, just because someone believes something doesn't mean it's true, right? Let me show you a few examples. Mormonism teaches that there are many gods, and, in fact, even you can become a god. But Christianity, Judaism and Islam teach that there is only one God. Islam teaches that Jesus was just a prophet, Jehovah's Witnesses say he was an angel, and Christianity says he is God. Hinduism and Buddhism teach that we will be reincarnated when we die, but Christianity, Judaism and Islam say we do not. Regarding salvation, those who say that "all paths/religions lead to God" are in direct contradiction to those who state "Jesus is the only way to salvation."

Either one doctrine is right (true) and the other is wrong (untrue), or both doctrines are false. They can't both be true because they are contradictory statements. This is not to say that all religions don't contain some truth. It just means that they may be correct in some teachings but wrong in their doctrine. For example, most religions teach that murder is wrong, but that doesn't mean that the doctrine of reincarnation is correct. While most of the major religions agree on some moral teachings, they have completely opposite doctrines that cannot be reconciled. They do not accurately represent all of reality.

Example: In the equation 4 + 4, the correct answer (truth/reality) is 8. The answer 10 is incorrect, but it's closer to the truth than an answer of 100. If Christianity is the truth, then Islam and Judaism, which are both monotheistic religions (religions that believe in one God), are closer to the truth in this one aspect or doctrine *than Hinduism and Buddhism, which are polytheistic (belief in many gods).*

Unfortunately, too many people live their entire lives without even realizing that they believe things that are contradictory. And often, their beliefs don't match their actions, which only goes to show that what is really true for them is what they act upon, not what they claim to believe. Example: A man might say he believes that when he dies he will have to answer for anything bad he did in his life, but then, hours later, he commits the very acts he just said he will be held accountable for. If he really believed he would be held accountable, he would act on that belief by not doing evil things. The truth, then, is that he doesn't really believe he will be held accountable, or if he does really believe it, he doesn't believe it enough to turn his beliefs into action.

So, since each religion is a truth claim, it is the responsibility of every human to examine those truth claims to discover which one best matches reality, then conform his/her life to that truth. We are very much like jurors in a court case. We must consider each hypothesis (religion) carefully, examine the evidence thoroughly, and base our conclusions on logic and research. If I reach the conclusion that Islam is true, then I want to change my life and become the best Muslim I can. If I believe that Buddhism is correct, then I want to be a great Buddhist, and if I come to the conclusion that there is no God, then I will become a sincere atheist.

The single most important question a person can answer in life is, "What is going to happen to you when you die?" The way you answer this question will determine how you should live your life.

Example: if evolution is true, then when I die I will cease to exist. Conclusion – I should get as much pleasure in this life as possible. If Hinduism is true, then when I die, I will be reincarnated based on my works. Conclusion – I should do good deeds to others so that I can erase my bad karma. If Christianity is true, then when I die I will face judgment, and only those who accepted Jesus' forgiveness will enter heaven. Conclusion – I should accept his forgiveness and live my life according to his commands.

My sons, don't wait to do this research for yourself. Life is short. Because this issue is so important, I implore you to put all of your effort into finding the answer. And it is my belief, that if you do so, you will come to the same conclusion that I have reached.

Once he had finished reading the last of the journal entry, Raptor turned off the hand-held device and put it back in his pocket. He hadn't meant to read the entire thing, but was surprised to find it so intriguing. He had heard people talk about religion and debate things back and forth, but he had never read anything that approached the topic from a foundational perspective. Despite his desire to blow off Steven's words, Raptor couldn't stop his mind from mulling them over and over. *You're an atheist*, the voice in his head repeated. *Yeah, but only by default. I've never really looked into what the other religions teach and why they believe it. But that's because I don't believe there's a God. Maybe if I did, it would make sense to research things. Evolution has proven that God isn't real. Everything came about by natural processes.*

Yet no matter how hard he tried to push the nagging thought away, it kept returning. *Are you sure about that? Steven's right, the question of what will happen after you die is the most important question in life, but you've never given it much thought.*

"Hey, Raptor. Did you drink some bad *juri*-juice or something?"

Xavier's words jolted Raptor out of his musings. "No. . .I'm fine. why?"

"Oh, I don't know," Xavier replied. "It's just I've never seen you just stare into space for a minute without blinking before. The stuff on those data drives must be pretty heavy indeed for it to have *that* kind of effect on you."

Raptor winced. "Yeah, I guess you could say it's 'heavy'." He paused for a second as he debated inwardly whether or not to say anything more. "Let me ask you something. You're a Christian, right?"

Xavier threw his boss a strange look before turning his attention back to the road. "Uh. . .sure. I guess you could call me that. But just for the record, I'm not one of those crazy, fundamentalist types. I believe in God, go to church once in awhile, say my Hail Mary's and go to confession. Why do you ask?"

Ignoring his question, Raptor continued. "Do you believe that Christianity is the truth and other religions are wrong?"

"Well. . .I wouldn't go that far," Xavier said as he cocked his head to the side and grimaced. "After all, who's to say that Christians have the monopoly on truth. It seems to make sense to me that as long as you're sincere, God will let you in."

"But can't you be sincerely *wrong* about something?" Raptor asked.

"Okay, so I guess I should say you have to be sincere about doing good deeds."

"Such as?"

"I don't know, give to the poor, help other people, don't be selfish. . .stuff like that," Xavier stated.

"So basically, just follow the Ten Laws," Raptor said.

Xavier let out a boisterous laugh. "The Ten Commandments, not the Ten Laws!"

Raptor grinned despite his mistake. "Yeah, the Ten Laws just doesn't have the same ring to it. By the way, take Coney Ave to the shop. I want to come in from the alley."

"Sure thing boss," Xavier said as he turned right onto the indicated street.

"Can you name any of them?" Raptor asked, resuming the conversation.

"What? The commandments?"

"Yeah."

Xavier thought for a moment before answering. "There's, 'You should not kill, You should not lie, You should not steal.' What's that other one. . .oh yeah, 'You should not cheat.' I don't remember the rest off the top of my head."

"So, do you keep the Ten Commandments?" Raptor asked.

The con man turned to stare at his employer. Based on the expression on his companion's face, Raptor could tell that he wasn't very thrilled with the turn the conversation had taken. "Why the sudden interest in my beliefs?" Xavier asked, dodging the question.

Raptor shrugged. "Don't worry, it's not that big of a deal. I was just curious."

Studying Raptor's face for a moment longer and seeing nothing more than honest curiosity, Xavier finally decided to answer. "I may not be the poster boy for Christianity, but I could be a lot worse. Take Charon's wacko brother, Marcel, for example. I mean, I can understand that the guy would get ticked off at us because we owe him ten-thousand dollars, but then he lies to us about the Nelson deal, cheats us out of our share, and then kills poor Collins just because he felt like it. I think in the grand scheme of things, when compared to guys like Marcel, I've got nothing to worry about."

"Is that part of the church's teachings? That as long as you're not as bad as other people, then you get into heaven?" Raptor asked. "Where do they draw the line? Is this teaching in the Bible?"

"Where is all of this coming from?" Xavier replied, his expression one of complete confusion. "Who are you, and what did you do with Raptor?"

Laughing lightly, Raptor stretched and let out a sigh. "I don't know. It's just something that Steven said that got me thinking. That's all."

"Steven? The big, bald, dark-skinned guy?"

Raptor nodded. "Yeah, that guy."

Xavier harrumphed. "I wouldn't take *anything* that guy says seriously. I mean, here's a guy who claims to be religious, yet cheats on his wife and takes her money to boot. What a hypocrite."

Raptor didn't respond as Xavier brought the truck to a stop in front of their 'base.' Raptor and his associates ran a marginally successful auto repair shop as a front to their criminal activities. The rectangular building that housed the shop consisted of a fairly large, front office section, several internal rooms and storage areas, plus the main auto shop in the back of the building, which had two large garage doors leading into it, one at each end. At least, that's what was visible to the average customer. But beneath the shop, the group had built an extensive network of rooms and hallways that were used for a variety of nefarious purposes. The entire building was surrounded by an eight-foot high, electromagnetic fence. Due to the fact that it was still early in the morning, the normal business crowd and employees had still not arrived, leaving the place deserted.

Giving a mental command via his wireless implant, Xavier opened the gate that allowed access to the back parking area, which contained a selection of hovercars and vans in various stages of repair. As they pulled into the lot, Raptor did his customary scan of the area to make sure that nothing was out of the ordinary. Xavier piloted the vehicle into one of the empty spaces near the back of the building, while Jade parked the hovervan in front of a smaller entrance next to the southern garage door that led into the vehicle bay. With both vehicles inside the lot, Xavier sent a command to the gate, causing it to close behind them.

Taking out his holoscreen once again, Raptor checked the feeds from the cameras mounted on the fence as a final precaution. Satisfied that the coast was clear, he gave Charon a mental command to move the prisoners into the building. Immediately, the side door of the van slid open and Charon herded the three blindfolded men out of the van and through the side entrance.

Once the prisoners were secured in one of the secret rooms below the building, Raptor assembled his team in one of the upstairs offices. Jade entered last, a flying animal that looked like a gray squirrel with leathery wings perched on her shoulder.

"It's just past seven o'clock, so we've got to make this quick. I want us out of here before the morning crew arrives," Raptor said, his tone business-like. "It turns out, we got more than we bargained for with our captives." For the next several minutes, Raptor related to the other three the conversation he had with Steven, as well as the information he gleaned from the stolen data. For now, he decided it was best to leave out all of the details about the prophecy and signs. Once he was finished, he looked at each of them in turn. "Since this isn't a normal job situation, I'd like each of your opinions before we take a vote on how to proceed. Do we turn them in and take the money to pay back Marcel, or do we help these guys try to find a way to Earth?"

Without hesitation, Charon spoke. "I don't trust these religious fanatics. We have no guarantees that anything they've said is true. They're probably lying about being able to stabilize the portals. Scientists have been trying to do that since the First Colony arrived in Tartarus. I say we turn 'em in, get our reward, and pay our debts."

Raptor studied Charon briefly, then nodded. "Anyone else have an opinion?"

Jade crossed her arms, a defiant look on her face. "I don't think the government would be offering such a large amount for these men unless they stole something very important. If *anything* they said is true, we can't just turn them in. You said that those documents looked legit, right?"

"Yes. Down to the governmental file numbers," Raptor confirmed.

"Then I say we take it as truth. I for one don't want to be turned into some walking zombie. And if there's even a slight chance we can get out of Tartarus, then I'm willing to do what I can to make that happen. I vote we help them."

All eyes turned toward Xavier, who held up his hands in surrender. "Look, I'm not sure what to think. Charon's got a point. I don't want his big, bad brother to string me up for robbing him. But then again, I don't much like the idea of being a mindless zombie either. So. . .I think I'll sit this one out."

"Well then, I guess you get to cast the deciding vote, O Illustrious Leader," Jade said, looking at Raptor.

Steven's cryptic words came rushing back to him. *". . .the lives of thousands rest in your hands, Tens of thousands will live or perish by your choices."* Feeling the weight of the decision, Raptor paused and closed his eyes in an attempt to clear his mind. Finally, he opened his eyes once more and faced the others.

"I think we should–"

His words were cut off by a loud, commanding voice that came through each of their wireless implants. "This is Inspector Hawkins of the Elysium Security Force! We have the building surrounded! Release your hostages now!"

Chapter 16

Negotiations

Raptor and his companions exchanged looks of shock mixed with confusion. "What?!" Charon exclaimed angrily. "How did they find us?"

"I. . .I don't know," Raptor said, a puzzled expression on his face.

"But I thought we had an 'agreement' with Mathison's people," Jade commented. "Why would he send Hawkins after us now?" Sensing her master's agitation, her winged pet let out a series of clicks and chirps.

"It has to have something to do with our 'hostages'," Xavier replied. "They probably followed those guys to their little hideout, but we beat them to the punch and captured them first. After that, they followed us here."

"Maybe. Then again, not all of Mathison's people know that we're on his payroll," Raptor said. "Whatever the case, we've now got to figure out what to do about this. Let me see if I can get a little more information about what's going on." Using the microphone imbedded in his lip, he mentally switched on his implanted commlink and began speaking. "Inspector Hawkins, this is Mahmoud Salib," Raptor said, using one of his aliases. Putting just the right amount of uncertainty in his voice, he continued. "We. . .uh. . .we don't know what you're talking about. My friends and I were just getting ready to open up the shop for the day. We don't. . .we don't know anything about any hostages."

He didn't have to wait long for a reply. "Don't play dumb with me, Raptor. We know you've got three hostages in there with you and your gang. We've already got enough against you to put you away for the rest of your life. I don't think you want to add the murder of three innocents to that do you? If you come along peacefully, you have my word that your coop-eration will be taken into consideration at your trial. Oh, by the way, don't even think of trying to sneak out through the 'secret' underground tunnel. We've got that covered as well."

All attempts at pretense gone, Raptor's voice returned to normal. "Well, then, Inspector, it appears that I don't have many options. Give me a couple of minutes to retrieve the hostages."

"NO. You get them out here now or we come in to get them!" Hawkins shouted.

"No need to get trigger happy," Raptor replied. "We'll have them out to you as soon as possible. They're locked in a room downstairs and it'll take us at least a minute to get down there, untie them, and get them back upstairs."

"Fine. But if I get the slightest hint that you're trying to pull something, we'll be on you before—"

"Understood." Raptor said, cutting him off. Returning his attention to his colleagues, he frowned. "The ESF aren't here for our 'hostages'. They're here because someone turned us in."

Charon swore violently. "Marcel!"

"Really?" Xavier asked in surprise. "But. . .what makes you so sure?"

"Several reasons," Raptor explained. "One, our dear inspector called Steven and his companions 'hostages' and said that they were 'innocents'. If he was after them for stealing from the government, he would've called them criminals, fugitives, or some other nasty word, and he most *definitely* wouldn't have referred to them as innocents."

"Unless he's deliberately trying to throw us off," Jade countered.

"But if he was, then by doing so he's giving us more power in the negotiations," Raptor replied. "The deaths of hostages are a lot worse for public relations than the death of a couple of fugitives. Second, and most importantly, he knows about our underground tunnel. Only one of our associates in the criminal networks would know about that exit. And, considering how Marcel feels about us right now, I think it makes the most sense that he's the one who turned us in."

"Okay, so what do we do, then?" Xavier asked, his anxiety slipping through his normally calm demeanor.

"I'm not sure yet," Raptor said. "But, I'm thinking we might be able to use the help of our 'hostages'. Charon, go bring them up here."

"We don't need them," Charon protested. "Why don't we just turn ourselves in? You know Mathison will get us off the hook."

"Because if we do, then we pretty much doom ourselves to becoming slaves of Mathison, casualties in a war, or both!"

"So you've just bought into everything Russell said, huh? Just like that."

"I trust what my own eyes have seen," Raptor retorted. "The data on that drive is real. We don't have time to waste right now. Just go get them!" Raptor commanded. Charon cast one last frustrated look at his friend before exiting the room.

A heavy silence hung in the air for several seconds. Finally, Raptor spoke. "Let's focus on putting together a plan. Any ideas?"

Xavier hesitated just a moment longer before responding. "Well, we've got those invisibility cloaks. Could we somehow use those?"

Raptor shook his head. "Maybe. The problem is, those only work under poor lighting conditions, unless your only goal is to hide but not move. We'll have to keep that in mind, though."

"Can we just use one of the cars in the shop to escape?" Jade suggested.

"None of those are running right now," Raptor said.

"What about that new weapon, or the Volt? Maybe we could use those?" Jade offered.

"I'm not sure we want to use that Vortex weapon," Raptor replied. "From what I've read, it seems like it might be unpredictable. But we'll definitely want to keep the Volt handy in case the ESF brought a Guardian with them. What we really need is to find out what we're up against in case it comes to a fight."

"Can't we just check the camera feeds?" Xavier asked.

"No. The ESF will have jammed them for sure," Raptor replied.

"What about Zei?" Jade suggested, nudging the flying mammal on her shoulder, causing it to coo softly.

Raptor grinned at the idea. "Yes. Send him out through the skylight and have him circle around the building a few times."

Nodding, Jade slipped out the door of the room to go release her flying pet. In the meantime, Raptor withdrew his holoscreen and activated it. As the two men waited, they heard the sounds of approaching feet. A moment later, Charon returned with Steven, Braedon and Gunther in tow. Although their hands were no longer bound and they were not blindfolded, Charon remained close behind them, his expression one of obvious distrust.

Turning to face the men, Raptor launched into a summary of the situation. "It seems that Charon's brother, Marcel, has turned us into the ESF. They have us surrounded, and our emergency exit is blocked. They want us to release our 'hostages', but they don't seem to realize exactly who it is we've captured."

"I'm sure they'll figure it out real quick if you *do* turn us over to them," Steven stated.

"Which is why we don't plan to," Raptor said. "I think it would be in all of our best interest if we work together on this. Are you with us?"

Although Braedon was clearly not happy about the prospect of working with known criminals, he understood that they didn't have any other choice. Steven gave him a reassuring glance, then replied, "Yes, we are. What do you have in mind?"

At that moment, Inspector Hawkin's voice came through Raptor's implant. "Time's up, Raptor."

The criminal leader glanced at each of the men assembled in the room. "I'm going to stall for time. Jade's releasing her *mindim*. As it flies around the outside of the shop, the microscopic camera imbedded in its head will allow us to see what we're up against. Charon, get the satchel containing the Vortex weapon and Volt. We might need those." As Charon exited the room, Raptor turned to Xavier. "Take off his inhibitor," he said, motioning toward Braedon. As the con artist reached over and removed the implant inhibitor from Braedon's temple, Raptor finally replied to the ESF officer.

"Listen carefully, Inspector," Raptor replied, "you can have the hostages, but you're going to have to let me and my colleagues go. If you or any one of your men tries to play the hero, then the evening holofeeds are going to be posting a story about how one of the precious ESF Inspectors failed in his negotiations with known criminals. These kind of things can be very damaging to an otherwise promising career."

Raptor paused to allow the threat to sink in. Suddenly, the holoscreen sprang to life with the images that were being transmitted from Jade's pet as it flew around the building. He studied them with interest even as he continued his conversation.

"Now, with that said, here's how this is going to work: I'm going to release two of the hostages to you. One of my men will accompany them to the south garage door. You will then allow him to enter the hovervan parked there and drive it into the vehicle bay. We'll leave the third hostage tied up inside the shop. Once we're all aboard the van, you'll allow us to drive it out of the lot. When we're safely out of the city, you can go in to retrieve the third hostage. But just so you know, we're leaving a little package with the last hostage. If you try to attack us, you'll find pieces of this shop blown halfway to the Governor's mansion. Got it, or do I need to repeat it for you?"

There was a long pause, causing Raptor to wonder if the man was going to go for it. Finally, the voice of the Inspector returned. "Understood. You know, of course, that this is just buying you a little time. We'll find you again."

Ignoring the man's boastings, Raptor shut off his microphone transmitter. The moment he did so, Braedon started berating him. "How is turning us over to the ESF going to help us? In case you don't remember, you said yourself that everyone in Elysium will probably recognize Gunther and I! I don't think that this Inspector will–"

"Don't presume to tell me what to do!" Raptor interrupted, his anger barely restrained. "I know what I'm doing. Now if you'll shut up for a minute, I'll explain the plan."

Hoping to prevent any further issues, Steven placed a calming hand on Braedon's shoulder. Taking a cue from his mentor, Braedon took a deep breath, then relaxed. "I apologize."

Somewhat taken aback by the man's response, Raptor found himself at a momentary loss for words. "Fine. Now, based on the images from Jade's *mindim*, there's a dozen men stationed outside: four covering each of the two garage doors, and another two pairs covering the front and side office doors.

"Based on the fact that the ESF got through the outside gate without raising any alarms, they must have been given the codes," Raptor continued. "That solidifies it in my mind that they were given info from Marcel. Which means, they were waiting to ambush us, but didn't count on the fact that we would have prisoners. This can work to our advantage. If we play our cards right, we can all avoid getting taken by the ESF."

Steven leaned in closer, curiosity lighting up his face. "Sounds good. What have you got in mind?"

Raptor gave his former mentor a lopsided grin. "Here's what we're going to do. . ."

****

"Here they come," the officer standing next to the Inspector said softly as the southern door of the shop opened.

It's about time, Inspector Jonathan Hawkins thought as the two hostages came into view. The Inspector was not a particularly brilliant man, but, like an expert gambler, he had a knack for being able to assess situations to determine exactly what to do in order to come out on top. Sometimes that meant bribing the right official at the right time, and sometimes it meant choosing the right side to be on in a fight. When he initially accepted this assignment, he thought maybe his intuition had been misguided. But with the appearance of hostages, he knew instantly that he had struck gold once more.

When most of his other colleagues had been assigned to look for the two fugitives, he had quickly volunteered to lead the force that would try to capture this small gang of criminals. He felt sure that he would have a better chance of getting his promotion if he could successfully bring in a gang, rather than wasting his time on some wild *endek* chase looking for fugitives who had probably fled the city. The arrest of the gang alone would have been impressive, but now, if he could bring in the gang *and* rescue three hostages, his promotion would be assured.

All he had to do was make sure everything went according to plan.

Lang and Haupt, move in and help the hostages, Hawkins commanded mentally. Nodding slightly in acknowledgement of the silent order, the men left their positions behind the hovercar that rested thirty feet to the left of the Inspector's own vehicle and moved cautiously toward the two prisoners.

As they moved in, Hawkins could see their escort, a handsome young man in his mid-twenties – whom the Inspector quickly identified as Xavier Traverse – step away from the hostages and climb into the nearby hovervan, as per the negotiated agreement. Hawkins leaned against the side of his car, his pistol tracking the man's movements in heightened anticipation to see if Traverse, or any of his team was attempting to alter the agreed-upon terms. So far, everything seemed to be proceeding appropriately. The hovervan's engine rumbled to life as the garage door leading into the shop opened. The large, mechanized door stopped with just enough room for the van to slip through. As Traverse pulled the vehicle inside the building, Hawkins scrutinized the interior, searching for any signs of attack, or any clues that might prove useful. However, the light cast by the Globe, which hung low in the east against the roof of the enormous cavern that housed the city, was unable to pierce the darkness of the southern-facing shop.

Once the van was enveloped by the shadows inside the building, Hawkins switched his attention to the two hostages that his officers were now escorting back to the safety of the far side of the police vehicle. Both men looked ragged and weary, and their clothes and faces were stained with dirt and grime, causing the Inspector to wonder how long they had been held captive, and under what conditions. Although the dark-skinned, older man looked strong for his age, his shoulders sagged and he leaned heavily on his left leg, indicating that his right was injured. The younger man's short-cropped hair, combined with his muscular build and steady gait gave Hawkins the impression that he had spent time in the military.

Narrowing his eyes, the Inspector frowned as the two officers returned to their position behind the car with the hostages. *Something looks familiar about that younger one,* he thought as he studied his features more closely. Suddenly it clicked, and his face lit up in shock. *The height! The hair! The build! It can't be!*

However, before Inspector Hawkins could even form another coherent thought, chaos exploded around him.

Several laser blasts that seemed to materialize out of thin air from somewhere near the garage opening struck the vehicle next to him, shattering the back window and causing shards of flying glass to imbed themselves in his face and neck. Reeling from the attack and from the resulting pain, Hawkins fell to the ground, his face feeling as if it were on fire due to the deep cuts from the glass. Moving into a sitting position with his back against the car, he glanced to his left to see the unconscious body of his partner slumped over the hood.

His mind finally recovering from the initial shock, he activated his wireless commlink. *Officer down! We're taking fire at the south entrance! Lang and Haupt, watch out for the. . .* His thought ended mid-sentence, for as he mentioned their names, he turned to look in their direction. It took a moment for his confused brain to register the horrible truth that his carefully laid plan was unraveling. Both officers lay unconscious on the ground. Their weapons were now in the hands of the former 'hostages' and were pointed in his direction. Before his mind could form another thought to warn the rest of his force, he saw a bright flash from one of the weapons and his world faded to black. . .

****

You've got two more officers coming toward your position around the east side of the building and another two coming from the west, Raptor warned via his implant. Braedon sent a quick acknowledgement back to the gang leader, then changed the frequency of his implant to communicate with the police force. *This is one of the hostages! Inspector Hawkins is down, as are the other three officers! Please help us! We're hiding behind the police car nearest to the gate.*

Rising up just enough so that he could see over the back of the vehicle, Braedon waved quickly to the two approaching officers that were even now cautiously making their way to the edge of the building, their weapons at the ready.

Where are the attackers? one of the officers asked Braedon silently.

I'm not sure, came his mental reply. *However, I don't see anyone now. The coast looks clear.*

Taking up a position at the edge of the building, the first officer covered the area with his pistol while his partner sprinted the fifty feet to the police vehicle. Once there, he knelt down to check on the fallen officers. As he did so, Steven knocked him unconscious with a well-placed blow to his head. In the same instant, Braedon stunned the other unsuspecting officer, dropping him to the ground with a single shot.

Meanwhile, the other two officers coming around the east side of the building arrived just in time to see their comrades fall unconscious. However, with their attention focused on the fact that their hostages were now hostile, they never noticed the bending of the light that signaled the existence of two cloaked figures that huddled close to the wall. Turning slightly so that the nozzles of their weapons protruded from the edge of the invisibility cloaks, Jade and Charon opened fire on the surprised policemen.

The other two are down, Charon reported.

Great! That just leaves the two guarding the front door, Raptor replied. *With any luck, we'll be out of here before they can cause any problems. But just in case, Jade and Braedon, set up watch at the corners. We're almost finished loading, then we'll get out of here. Charon and Steven come back inside and help us finish up.*

Braedon sent another short acknowledgment, then filled Steven in on the plan. Within moments, Braedon and Jade were in position and Steven and Charon had disappeared into the darkened interior of the shop.

Suddenly, an explosion coming from within the building knocked Braedon and Jade off their feet. Shaking his head in an attempt to ward off the aftereffects of the shock, Braedon recovered and stood up, using the wall for support. He noticed as he did so, that Jade was also back on her feet heading toward the garage door from the opposite side.

Reaching the large opening seconds after the martial arts expert, Braedon stared into it, his eyes taking a moment to adjust to the darkness. When they did, he felt his stomach tighten in fear. The bodies of Steven and Charon lay unmoving on the debris-strewn floor, several paces from the side of the hovervan. The vehicle's engine was still running and the sliding side door stood ajar.

But although Braedon's mind registered all of those things, his attention was fully captured by the scene unfolding to his left in the doorway that led to the offices. Raptor was being held aloft several feet in the air by a massive hand that had him gripped around the throat. Attached to that hand and the arm that supported it was the seven-foot tall, muscular form of a Type II Guardian. A Hybrid!

Chapter 17

The Second Sign

At the sight of the newcomers, the genetically-altered soldier twisted his longer-than-average neck in their direction. As a soldier in the employ of the government of Elysium, Braedon had encountered specimens of each of the three types of Guardians before. And each time, he had been both impressed and repulsed by the blending of human and animal traits that comprised the Type II and Type III versions. In this case, the part-animal portion of the Guardian's DNA appeared to come from that of a reptile. The man's face, while mostly human-looking, had the slightly-elongated snout of a reptile, and was covered with dark-brown scales instead of skin. Although the rest of the man's large, muscular body was concealed by the black, skin-tight armor worn by the Guardians, Braedon guessed that the rest of his body was similarly covered by scales. When on covert missions, the Hybrids often wore matching black helmets to hide their features. However, when in combat, they sometimes removed them in order to allow their disturbing appearance to shock and intimidate their opponents.

And based on Jade's expression, it was working.

The martial arts expert seemed rooted to the spot, her gaze held by the blood-red, reptilian eyes that stared back at her across the shop. As the Guardian studied Jade and Braedon, the man's grotesque expression split into a grin, allowing his forked tongue to shoot out of his mouth and move rapidly over his razor-sharp teeth.

With a seemingly effortless motion, the Hybrid tossed Raptor aside, sending him crashing to the ground near the van. The Guardian's sudden movement served to awaken Jade and Braedon from their stupor. Recovering their wits, the two raised their weapons almost simultaneously and opened fire. Expecting their attack, the genetically-altered man leapt to the side with such speed that both Braedon and Jade momentarily lost sight of their prey. Then, in one swift motion, the Guardian dove toward them and knocked the pistol out of Jade's hand. A moment later, the half-human switched directions and rolled toward Braedon.

Leaping backward, Braedon managed to get off several shots from his laser pistol, two of which found their mark. However, whether due to the black armor or the man's own scaley skin, the shots seemed to have little effect. Having closed the distance between them, the Guardian came out of his roll and kicked out with his left leg, sweeping the feet out from under Braedon and sending him crashing to the grease-stained floor.

With the loss of her weapon, Jade threw off her invisibility cloak and moved in to attack the man with the skills honed by many years of training. Jade launched into a series of attacks that would have killed a normal man. Yet despite her skill and power, it became immediately apparent that Jade was no match for the Guardian. With a nearly two-foot height advantage and increased agility, the man was able to block most of the blows. The ones that did manage to slip through his defenses merely served to aggravate him as they bounced harmlessly off his armor.

Getting back to his feet, Braedon joined in the melee, hoping that his stronger frame and taller stance would serve to keep the man off balance. At first, his plan seemed to work as the Guardian backpedaled away from his two attackers. But then, the reptilian Hybrid suddenly went on the offensive, the man's powerful blows sending Jade and Braedon reeling. Loosing her footing on the rubble strewn across the floor, Jade fell hard on her left side. Kicking out with his foot, the Guardian connected with her stomach, doubling her over in pain. With one attacker down, the genetically-enhanced soldier focused his attention on Braedon and, with a series of powerful blows, knocked him to the floor. Taking advantage of his opponent's momentary weakness, the Guardian prepared to crush Braedon's ribcage with a single, well-placed kick.

However, at that moment a winged creature flew into the man's face, its claws digging at his scaly hide. The sudden assault from Jade's *mindim* caused the Guardian to step backward and crash into one of the many racks of car parts and tools. Howling in pain as several of the heavy items fell on top of him, he flailed his arms around in an attempt to strike the annoying creature. But after its initial attack, the *mindim* wisely flew out of range and came to rest on one of the overhead beams supporting the roof.

Jade, we have to find a weapon! Braedon called out to her mentally, hoping that perhaps she would be able to recover quickly enough to help him. *I'll try to hold him off while you—*

Before Braedon could finish the thought, the Guardian regained his balance and lunged toward him. Braedon knew immediately that, up to this point, the man had been playing with them – enjoying the exercise. But the pain from the tools and the *mindim's* attack had put an end to the Hybrid's "good mood."

Braedon tried desperately to get out of the way, but to no avail. The Guardian's body slammed into his side, the momentum sending the two combatants flying several feet across the floor toward the center of the room. The force of the blow caused Braedon to momentarily black out. When he recovered moments later, he opened his eyes to see the grotesque, reptilian face staring down at him. However, to Braedon's surprise, a pained expression filled the man's face and the red, slitted eyes were looking upward. Only when the Guardian rolled off of Braedon and fell sideways onto the ground did he understand what had happened.

Steven was clinging to the man's back, his arm wrapped around the Guardian's neck in a choke-hold. Using his larger size and greater strength to his advantage, the Hybrid rolled until Steven was beneath him. With his opponent struggling for breath, the half-human grabbed Steven's hand and gripped the pinky finger of his right hand tightly and pulled it backward. Howling in pain, Steven instantly let go of the man. Wanting desperately to go to the aid of his mentor and friend, yet unable to convince his bruised and battered body to move, Braedon watched in horror as the Guardian leapt to his feet, lifted Steven into the air, and hurled him onto the front hood of a nearby hovercar that rested on a repair lift. The front windshield shattered with a loud crash as Steven's body slammed into it.

Adrenaline coursing through his veins, Braedon let out a feral cry as he forced his weary body to respond. Rising unsteadily to his feet, he grabbed a large wrench that had fallen to the floor near him and threw it at the Guardian. Reacting swiftly, the man blocked the object with a swipe of his arm. However, the distraction was just enough to allow Raptor, who had recovered from his initial encounter with the Hybrid, a chance to get in close enough to hit the man in the back of his legs with a heavy, metal pipe.

Although Raptor's blow should have broken the Guardian's bones, his armor absorbed much of the damage, causing him to merely stumble and fall to his knees. Leaping forward, Raptor prepared for another strike when a laser blast suddenly shot across the room from the door on the north wall and struck his left arm. Reeling sideways from the impact, Raptor lost his grip on the metal bar and fell to the ground.

Turning his head in the direction of the attack, Braedon watched as the last two police officers entered the building. With the two newcomers along the north wall, and the Guardian standing in the center of the room, Braedon knew with a dreaded certainty that it was over. They had lost.

Staring around the room, Braedon searched frantically for signs of the others, hoping that perhaps Charon, Jade or Xavier would have a weapon they could use. However, Charon still lay unmoving near the southern door, and Jade was still curled into a fetal position on the floor as she struggled to recover from the Guardian's kick. Xavier, whose unconscious body was still in the driver's seat of the van which was parked near the eastern wall of the shop, was just beginning to stir.

No one was in a position to help - no one, except the last person Braedon expected - Gunther.

The side door of the van suddenly slid sideways, revealing the figure of the scientist. In his hands was the Vortex weapon, which he pointed directly at the two police officers. With hands that shook violently, Gunther braced himself and pulled the trigger on the rifle-like gun.

But instead of the typical, loud crack of a ballistic projectile or laser beam, the Vortex produced what sounded like a rushing wind as it emitted a narrow cone of particles that completely missed the intended targets and instead hit the northern wall of the shop between the two police officers. The attention of everyone in the room became instantly fixated on the spiraling cone as it began to grow in size. The two officers began backing slowly away from the expanding circle of energy as it grew in intensity.

Suddenly, the ring of particles, which had now reached almost four feet in diameter, exploded outward, knocking everyone off of their feet, including Gunther. As he fell, he released the trigger of the weapon, shutting off the continuous stream. To his utter surprise and horror, the cone disappeared, but the circle of particles remained.

Only now, they had transformed into a miniature black hole.

Without warning, everyone and everything in the room began to be pulled toward the swirling vortex. Letting out cries of terror, the two police officers were lifted off of their feet and flew toward the tear in space. As they reached the center, their bodies twisted and contorted unnaturally, until finally, they disintegrated and disappeared.

Reacting quickly, the Guardian, who had been standing in the center of the room, looked around frantically for something to hold on to. Catching sight of a grate in the floor used to collect spilled fluids, the reptilian hybrid leapt toward it. However, the pull of the vortex threw off his aim, and his gloved hands fell short of their mark. Clawing frantically at the smooth concrete, the Guardian let out a terror-filled growl as he was inexorably drawn closer and closer to the hole that was now surrounded by swirling debris. Letting out a final cry, the Guardian's body contorted as it too was torn apart by the gravitational forces.

Although all of their opponents were gone, none of the others even noticed, for at that moment they were all desperately fighting to keep themselves from meeting the same fate. Horrified by what his actions had created, Gunther dove back into the interior of the hovervan and closed the door, as if shutting out the sight of the miniature black hole would somehow make it disappear. Xavier, who had now come to full consciousness, reacted to the appearance of the anomaly by firing up the engine of the van and inching the vehicle away from the vortex, the machine straining against the pull.

Gradually, Xavier was able to move the floating hovervan between his friends and the hole. With the majority of the gravitational pull deflected by the vehicle, Jade, Braedon, and the now conscious Charon were able to let go of the various stable objects that they had been latched onto and make their way to the side of the van.

Throwing open the side door facing away from the rip in time and space, Xavier called out to them. "Get in! Quick! I think that thing's building up steam! Pretty soon we won't be able to get away at all!"

Charon and Jade both complied without hesitation. Braedon, however, paused at the entrance to the door, his eyes fixed on the body of Steven, which still lay atop the vehicle twenty feet to their right. Because the car he had landed on faced the south and the vortex was against the north wall, the bulk of the car prevented the gravitational forces from ripping Steven's body from its resting place. But that wouldn't last long. Soon, both the car and the man would be gone.

"We've got to help Steven!" Braedon called out over the noise of the swirling winds.

"And what about Raptor?" Jade said from beside him as she stared out the window on the left side of the vehicle. "Look! He's not going to make it!"

Following her gaze, Braedon could see that Raptor had somehow managed to grab onto the grate in the floor that the Guardian had unsuccessfully attempted to reach before being sucked into the vortex. However, everyone in the vehicle could see that Raptor's strength was just about spent. His face was ashen, and the knuckles on his hands were white from the strain, and from the pain from his recent gunshot wound. The gravitational pull from the vortex, which was only twenty feet from where he lay on the ground, was now so powerful that Raptor's body was being lifted slightly into the air.

Help. . .me! Raptor cried out through his implant, his lips pursed tightly together as he struggled to hold on.

But before anyone could react, the criminal leader's fingers lost their hold.

Letting out a panicked cry, Raptor flailed his arms help-lessly, desperate to grab onto something as his body slid rapidly along the floor toward the hungry vortex. Unexpectedly, Raptor's body, which had been heading feet first toward the opening, suddenly swung around as if something had grabbed his leg. Startled, Raptor cried out again, his head now less than ten feet from the black hole.

Unsure of what had happened, he looked down to see that, miraculously, his left pant leg had snagged on the handle of a screwdriver that had somehow become wedged in the grate. The twisting of his body and subsequent twisting of the fabric had served to strengthen the material enough to keep it from ripping further. His forward momentum now arrested, Raptor turned to look in the other direction, his gaze staring into the gaping hole in front of him.

As he watched in fascinated horror, the vortex began to change. The outer, swirling edges started to loose their circular shape, while the inner core began to alternate between bulging and shrinking. Then, with a spectacular flash of brilliant color, the rip in time and space was gone.

Chapter 18

Passing the Flame

An eerie, unnatural silence was left in the wake of the disappearance of the vortex. The last of the loose papers and other lightweight materials that had been caught in the swirling winds had settled to the ground before any of the survivors moved or even dared to breathe. At last, their shock dissolving with the last traces of the vortex, the occupants of the hovervan began to stir.

Raptor. . .are. . .are you okay? Jade asked mentally, her mind finally reengaging.

When he failed to reply, Jade cautiously opened the side door of the van, her eyes fixed on the spot where the miniature black hole had appeared a minute ago, as if she feared it would return at any moment. When it didn't, she climbed out of the vehicle and made her way over to her employer and friend. Kneeling down next to him, she searched for any signs of injury. Seeing none, she leaned over him and put her face close to his.

"Raptor?" she said softly. Although he was still breathing, his vacant stare and pale face made it appear as if he were a corpse. "Raptor!" she said more loudly as she shook him gently. After two more attempts, he suddenly blinked rapidly and inhaled deeply. His eyes frantically scanned his surroundings before finally coming to rest on Jade.

"I'm. . .I'm still alive," he managed at last. "Steven. . .said this would happen! It's the second sign!"

"Calm down," Jade said, unnerved by the wild look in Raptor's eyes. "Are you hurt?" she said as Charon and Xavier approached.

"What?" Raptor asked in confusion, as if hearing her for the first time. "No. Nothing serious."

"Glad to hear it," Charon interjected, one of his thick hands holding a shop rag against a cut on his forehead, "because I've got this nagging feeling that this place is about to become very popular real soon."

"Unbelievable!" Xavier exclaimed as he knelt down next to Raptor to examine the tool that had saved his life. "You are one lucky *gorgejumper*. I mean, what are the odds that this screwdriver would happen to be just the right width, get wedged into this grate at just the right angle, your body would travel at just the right trajectory, and that it would get caught in just the right spot on your pant leg? Maybe we should go buy you a lottery ticket, because today must be your lucky day!"

Xavier fully expected his comment to elicit a wry grin from his friend or at least lighten his mood considerably by helping him to see how fortunate he was. Instead, he was completely taken off guard by the fearful, almost terrified expression that suddenly appeared on Raptor's face.

"C'mon, let's get moving," Charon stated as he helped Raptor to stand, the big man completely missing the exchange. Despite his strength and size, Charon himself had to fight to remain standing due to his recent injuries even as he helped Raptor to begin walking toward the van. "I see now why Mathison's goons were keeping news of that Vortex weapon so hush-hush. Just think what even one of those weapons could do to an army!"

Arriving at the vehicle, Raptor stood upright, his countenance reverting to its normal, business-like expression. "I'm okay," he pronounced to Jade and Charon as he stood without their aid. "Is everyone else alright?"

"Other than a stiff neck and a couple of new bruises, I think I'll live," Xavier said as he massaged his neck and grimaced.

"Nothing we can't handle," Charon said. "What's our next move?"

A sudden call from across the room instantly drew their attention in that direction. "Steven's still alive! Someone give me a hand!"

Without hesitation, Raptor began heading toward the damaged car, the others following a moment later. Braedon and Gunther were bent over the body of Steven and were removing as much of the broken glass as they could without injuring him further. As Raptor approached, Braedon exchanged glances with him, their mutual admiration of Steven creating a bond of understanding.

"He's cut up pretty bad, and I think he's got some broken bones," Braedon stated, the inflection of his voice grim.

Quickly assessing the situation, Raptor glanced back over his shoulder at Charon and Xavier, who were still several steps away. "Go get two of the police cars and bring them in here. Grab a couple of their jackets while you're at it," he commanded. Without replying, the two men nodded and jogged toward the open garage door. Returning his attention to his former mentor, Raptor reached up and felt the man's pulse. "It's faint, but he still might have a chance if we can get him out of here."

"But where will we go?" Braedon asked in concern. "We can't just take him to a hospital."

"We've got some friends who could help," Raptor said. "Jade and Gunther, go back to the van and get our gear and supplies. When Xavier and Charon pull the cars in here, load them up. Braedon, that shelf looks like it's adjustable. Grab it, and we'll use it as a gurney."

Together, the two men took the sturdy metal shelf, which had been emptied by the vortex, and detached it from the shelving unit. Laying it on the ground in front of the car, they gingerly removed Steven's unconscious body from the broken glass, lifted him carefully off of the car, and laid him down on the shelf. Noting the amount of blood on the side of his mentor's head, Braedon's concern was heightened anew. With their patient secured, the two men slowly lifted the makeshift gurney and carried it over to the police car that Xavier had just parked a couple of feet away. Opening up the back door, Raptor climbed inside. Together, the two men eased the shelf down on the back seat.

In a matter of minutes, the six companions had the two police hovercars loaded. Xavier and Jade donned two of the police jackets that they had commandeered from the unconscious officers still lying outside in the yard and climbed into the front seats of the first vehicle, Jade's pet *mindim* flying down to land on her lap, where it curled itself up into a ball. Gunther, playing the role of 'prisoner', sat in the back. Raptor and Charon put on the other two jackets and got into the second vehicle, while Braedon sat in the back seat in order to minister to Steven's wounds with a med kit they had taken from the collected gear.

As the two stolen vehicles exited the shop and headed toward the open gate, the sounds of approaching police sirens wailed throughout the city. *Xavier, follow my lead. I'm going to take a few back roads until Inspector Hawkin's backup is behind us,* Raptor said via his implant. After sending a quick acknowledgement, Xavier pulled his car behind Raptor's as the criminal leader led the way down a narrow alley, closing the gate surrounding the shop after them.

Before long, the echoing sirens were behind them. *We're not out of this yet,* Raptor communicated to the other vehicle. *It might attract attention if you follow me directly. Stay here for a minute or two, then pull out onto the main street. Meet us three blocks from The Pit. We'll ditch the police cars, take the secret tunnels to The Pit, and get some help for Steven. After that, we'll grab one of the Cliffjumpers parked there and head on over to The Vagabond Hotel. Aaron owes us anyway, so it shouldn't be too hard to convince him to give us some rooms where we can lay low for tonight. Tomorrow we'll get out of the city and figure out our next move.* With their plan in place, Raptor cautiously pulled his vehicle into the flow of traffic, his senses alert for any pursuit.

In the back of the car, Braedon had begun cleaning the extensive wounds on Steven's body, the sight of every newly discovered cut or abrasion intensifying Braedon's prayers. Doing his best in the cramped quarters of the back of the police car, Braedon grabbed a syringe filled with liquid stimulant and shot it into Steven's arm. After several minutes, he began to stir and moan, signaling his return to consciousness.

"Hang in there, Steven. We're going to get you some help soon," Braedon pleaded, his voice hushed. "I've given you some stim, which should stabilize your condition."

Steven's eyes fluttered open, and, after several seconds of disorientation, his gaze finally fixed on the familiar face sitting on the edge of the seat next to him. "Where. . .where are we?" he asked, his voice nothing more than a throaty whisper.

"We're safe, for now," Braedon answered.

"The Guardian?"

"Gone," Braedon said simply. "We escaped in two borrowed police cars. Don't talk. You need to save your strength."

Steven shook his head. "It's over for me, Braedon. My fight is over."

Although Braedon wanted to offer some reassurance to the contrary, he couldn't deny what was clearly evident.

"Find the way. . .back to Earth," Steven said, his breathing labored. "And. . .please. . .please try to save my. . .my family, if you can. Tell them. . .I'm sorry, and. . .and I love them."

Braedon ignored the rivulets of tears that ran unchecked down his face. "I will. I promise."

Steven closed his eyes for a moment as a wave of pain passed through his broken body. Opening them once more, he returned his gaze to Braedon, his eyes glazed and unfocused. "Raptor?" he managed.

"He's here, driving the car."

"You must. . .you must help him," Steven said. "God has a. . .a purpose for his life. Put your feelings aside. He is lost. . .like we once were." Pausing to gather his strength, he continued. "Be patient. He has many. . .many stumbling blocks preventing him from. . .taking the path that. . .leads to the. . .Gospel. His personal pain. . .and anger towards God runs deep. . .deeper than you could imagine. Let the Holy Spirit guide. . .your actions. . .and your speech."

Grief overwhelming him, Braedon could do nothing more than listen and mourn as his mentor, friend, and surrogate father faded.

Summoning one last ounce of strength, Steven spoke again, "Remember what I taught you. Raptor has. . .many of the same questions you once had. But, keep in mind. . .that. . .your goal is. . .is to win him to Christ,. . .not win a debate. Let your character. . .reinforce your words."

With his last instruction given, Steven closed his eyes, the lines in his aged face relaxing. "I'm. . .ready. . ., Lord. . ."

Releasing his last breath, the spirit that was Steven Russell departed, leaving behind nothing more than a broken, empty shell.

Chapter 19

The Nightmare

*H*is vision was shrouded in darkness. Disoriented, the man reached out with his arms to feel his way. To his left, he felt nothing but air. To his right. . .his fingertips brushed against cold, hard stone. Bringing his left arm around to join his right, he laid his palms against the wall. He leaned his body against the rough, durable surface, its permanence like a lifeboat to a drowning man.

Feeling his way along the wall, he moved slowly forward, searching for. . .something. . .anything. Where was he? Why couldn't he see? Was he blind, or was his vision gone because of a lack of light?

And why did he have this intense feeling that he was being hunted?

Suddenly, he froze in place, his heart thumping painfully against his ribcage. Was it his imagination playing tricks on him, or had he really heard a growl? In answer to his unspoken question, the sound repeated itself, only with greater volume. He HAD heard a growl! Whatever creature was producing that horrid rumble seemed hungry. And worse, it was getting closer!

Moving with renewed urgency, the man continued on blindly, his feet shuffling along the uneven floor. His breaths came fast and shallow as panic began to set in. Then, to his surprise, his eyes began to see a faint light coming from somewhere in front of him. With each step he took, it became brighter and brighter. Hope spurring him on, he ran as fast as he dared down what he could now see was some kind of tunnel or cave. Another growl erupted behind him, causing him to stumble in fright. Picking himself back up, he ran on toward the light.

The tunnel emptied unexpectedly into a large cavern made out of a strange type of rock that glowed with a dark-purplish hue. In the center of the cavern was the object that was producing the light. The man paused momentarily in shock. An ornate, jewel-encrusted sword stood erect atop a shining, two-foot high pedestal, its blade thrust halfway into the solid granite. Multi-colored, crystaline light radiated from the hilt and pommel, as if the weapon were alive.

However, despite the sheer beauty and wonder of the sword, the man recoiled. Something within him knew that to touch that weapon would be folly. Yet something within him also knew with an unmistakable certainty that wielding the blade was his only hope for defeating the beast that hunted him.

A deafening roar from behind sent him tumbling to the ground, terror piercing his heart. Turning, he cowered at the sight of the two, blood-red eyes that stared back at him. An enormous shadow detached itself from the blackness of the tunnel entrance. Although the man's eyes couldn't make out the details of the creature's form, its outline revealed horns, wings, and a serpentine body.

Terror unlike anything the man had ever known robbed him of his senses. He began to weep uncontrollably as he collapsed onto the cold, stone floor. After several precious seconds, one thought pierced through the *fog that clouded his mind. The sword! He had to reach the sword!*

The sound of the beast approaching infused his body with one last burst of energy, just enough to overcome the paralyzing fear. Crawling on his hands and knees, he headed toward the weapon. Yet the closer he got to it, the more he felt the pain of the blinding radiance that emanated from it.

It was too pure. He was unworthy to wield it. Defeated, the man curled into a ball and wept, his anguish bursting forth from his very soul.

Shutting his eyes tightly, he cried out in despair. Behind him, he heard the beast begin to laugh – a horrible, throaty laugh of triumph. The heat of the creature's fetid breath washed over the man, causing him to retch from the foul stench of brimstone. The monstrous shadow paused, as if relishing its victim's suffering. The man let out one last, shrill scream of terror as the beast opened its toothy maw and started to feed on its prey. . .

****

Raptor let out a strangled cry as he sat bolt upright in the hotel room bed, droplets of sweat beading on his forehead. He remained motionless for several seconds as he calmed his rapidly-beating heart.

"The nightmare again, huh?" Charon said from the other side of the darkened room. Although his voice was groggy from having just been awakened, his concern for his friend was still clearly evident.

Glancing over at the other bed, Raptor tried his best to shake off the nagging sense of dread and unease that always accompanied the dream. Disoriented, he tried to focus his mind on reviewing the day's events, hoping the mental exercise would serve to chase away the remaining vestiges of the nightmare.

After escaping from the shop, Raptor and the others had followed his plan and rid themselves of the police cars. Since Steven had already died by that time, they didn't have the added burden of seeking help for his injuries. Instead, they immediately grabbed one of the vehicles that Raptor and his criminal companions had hidden around the city at various safe houses and headed straight for the Vagabond hotel. With the help of their contact, Aaron, they were all settled down discretely for the night. Once arrangements had been made for getting Steven's body back to his family, Raptor collapsed onto his bed, letting exhaustion carry him into a fitful sleep. That is, until the nightmare occurred.

"Yeah," he replied simply, hoping his friend would drop the subject. However, Charon didn't seem to pick up on the hint.

"Look, Rahib, you've got to figure out what's causing this. We've known each other since before we were teens, yet I've never seen you like this. Even when we met, when you were still screwed up by whatever had happened to make you run away from home, you were never this disturbed. It's like. . .like some kind of mental attack. I'm startin' to think that Mathison's goons have come up with more than just a new physical weapon. Think about it, what if they could use that blasted *Pandora's Box* implant to put a nightmare into your head? It has certainly been robbing you of sleep and keeping you more on edge."

Raptor studied his friend for a moment before replying. "Hmmm. . .maybe," he said, trying again to brush off the subject.

"That has to be it," Charon continued. "Either that or there's some glitch with your implant. I've read of that happening. There's this guy once who had to be locked up because he kept seeing images from a video game he played in the *Box*.

He tried to kill the people around him because he thought he was still in the game. The doctors said that there was a problem with the implant."

"Great. So you're saying I'm crazy?" Raptor asked, his voice reflecting only partial sarcasm.

"Crazier than a cliffdiver jumping into the Well," Charon replied with a grin.

The two shared a brief chuckle before Raptor's mood turned serious once again. Several seconds of awkward silence passed before Raptor spoke. "I don't know, Caleb," he said, using Charon's real name. "Do you. . .You don't. . .Why do you think humans were brought through the portals here to Tartarus? Do you think there's someone, or something, like the Celestials that are pulling the strings?"

Charon frowned as he gazed at his friend. "Something really *does* have you spooked. That's a mighty big question to be asking at eleven-thirty at night."

"Yeah, you're right. Just forget it," Raptor said as he started to lie down again on the bed. To his surprise, Charon continued the conversation.

"I don't really know, and frankly, I don't really care. If the Celestials do exist, then I've never seen any proof of them. I guess the idea of aliens transporting select people from Earth to preserve the human race because some huge catastrophe is coming makes about as much sense as any of the other theories I've heard. But as with all such beliefs, they're just that: beliefs. There's no evidence for any of it."

"What about God?" Raptor asked, thankful for the darkness that served to conceal the tormented expression from his friend.

Silence hung in the air for so long that Raptor had begun to wonder if Charon had even heard his question. "What's going on, Rahib? You know where I stand, and I thought I knew where you stood. I don't believe for a second that there's some 'all-powerful' father God sitting on his golden throne just waiting to squash mankind if they don't follow his commands. All of the religions are just man-made superstitions that are used by con men to get people to obey them. It's all a power grab. Why would you even ask me such a question? And why would you bring it up? Does it have something to do with your nightmare?"

Raptor leaned his back against the wall as he sighed. "Yeah, you're right. It was a stupid question. It's just. . .something Steven said back at the Crimson Liberty hideout."

Charon's frown deepened. "I thought so. You looked. . .rattled when we were leaving. What did he say?"

Raptor paused. He debated inwardly how much to tell Charon. He'd been friends with Caleb for twenty years, and although they didn't always see eye to eye, they had shared many experiences together. If it came down to it, Raptor would give his life for him. But his hesitation in telling him about the prophecy stemmed from the fact that they shared a difference of opinion about Steven. Raptor still felt as if Charon hadn't fully forgiven him for running off to join the military when he was sixteen. Charon always blamed Steven for taking away his best friend, and he was actually happy when Raptor was accused of murder and had to drop out of the academy.

In the end, he decided to divulge his secret and take whatever response Charon gave with a grain of salt. "When we were talking about the Vortex and Mathison, Steven suddenly became. . .weird, as if he was hearing someone else's voice. He then began speaking cryptically, as if reciting a poem."

"What?" Charon said incredulously. "I told you. I never have understood why you ever gave that guy any respect. He's a religious nut. I certainly hope you're not giving any weight to anything he said in that poem. What was it about?"

Although Raptor could remember every word of the prophecy, as if it were etched forever on his heart, he decided to merely summarize it. "He said something about the fate of tens of thousands resting in my hands. He said that my fate was bound to theirs, and 'Only by opening the door to a new life would my own be saved', or something along those lines."

"See! That's exactly what I was just saying," Charon replied in irritation as he got up from the bed, flipped on a small lamp and poured himself a drink. "He was trying to control you by using religion. 'God says you should do this, and if you don't, bad things will happen.'"

Listening to the way Charon described the situation, Raptor suddenly felt his face flush from embarrassment. When he had been under Steven's tutelage, he *had* respected him. He had respected his physical prowess and skill. He had respected his intelligence and wit. And he had respected his strength of character. Raptor had never admitted this to Charon, but Steven had become like a surrogate father to him during those six years in the military.

But Steven had changed since then. He still respected his physical skill and intelligence, but his character had come under attack, and even more, he had joined a group that was labeled as religious terrorists and extremists. Should he believe Steven's explanation, or Charon's assessment? What was the truth?

The truth. There was that word again. Raptor thought back to Steven's journal entry. What was the truth?

"There's more," Raptor said at length, brushing off the nagging question.

"Yep, I knew it. Let me guess, it's something bad."

Raptor nodded. "He made a prophecy that I would have one standard month left to live unless I opened the doorway."

Charon shook his head in frustration as he swore. "That just ticks me off. I know you thought highly of the guy, but to try to use you like that just disgusts me. Well, let me tell you something: he was full of it! You definitely shouldn't be letting something like that bother you. And frankly, I think we should wash our hands of this whole stinking situation. I still think we should turn in soldier-boy and grandpa. We

could get the reward money *and* sell that Vortex weapon on
the black market. We could pay off my idiot brother, and still
have enough left over to live comfortably for awhile. It's a no-
brainer in my book."

Swinging his legs over the edge of the bed, Raptor faced
his friend. "I would agree with you, were it not for a couple
of things. First, I've read the documents that Braedon and
Gunther retrieved, and I'm convinced they're legit. Second,
you know as well as I do that these guys aren't lying. You can
tell just by looking at them. Gunther is totally out of his league
and would have been caught long ago were it not for Braedon.
And third, Steven gave me two signs that would prove that his
words were true."

Charon's body suddenly stiffened, leaving Raptor with no
doubt that his words had surprised his friend. "What signs?"
he said coldly.

"The first, he said, was already given," Raptor continued.
"He said that I would have a recurring nightmare. And before
you say anything, let me tell you that Steven described the
dream in detail."

Charon's eyes narrowed. "How many people have you told
about this nightmare besides me?"

"No one," Raptor stated. "It's not something I care to
share with others."

Although Charon remained stony and expressionless,
Raptor had known him long enough to tell that he was fighting
his own unease. "What was the second sign?"

Raptor took a deep breath, then plunged ahead. "He said
that God would demonstrate his power by saving my life
before the day was done."

Charon's head snapped around to look at Raptor in shock.
"This had better not be some messed up joke you're pulling on
me. If it is, I swear you'll regret it."

Raptor chuckled, despite the seriousness of their conversation. "I only wish it were a joke," he said. "Do you see

now why I'm a little on edge? Xavier said it earlier. What are the odds that that screwdriver would get jammed in that grate at just the right angle, and my pant leg would get snagged at just the right spot? It certainly messes with your head. I keep telling myself that it's just a coincidence, but it defies logic." For a moment, Raptor considered telling Charon about the line in the prophecy that mentioned the pain from his past, but decided against it. There were some things that were just too personal to mention, even to his best friend.

Although it was clearly apparent that Charon was disturbed by what he had just been told, he pretended to shrug it off as inconsequential. Downing the last of his drink, he turned to face Raptor. "Look, the man that you once respected as your teacher had changed. You need to accept that. For whatever reason, he felt he needed to scare you to get you to help open the portals back to Earth. Somehow, he was able to plant these nightmares into your head. After all, even *he* said that the implants could be used to control people. How much easier would it be to put a recurring dream there? And the fact that you had the dream before today means that he has been planning on involving you for some time. *That* could mean that this whole thing is some elaborate trap, which only reinforces my argument that we have nothing to do with it."

"But how could Steven possibly set up a way of saving my life that can only be explained as miraculous?" Raptor countered.

"I don't know," Charon said, the whole conversation beginning to wear on his nerves. "He was probably working with Hawkins and planned some other way to 'save your life' that he could pass off as being 'God's intervention,' but the unplanned screwdriver incident ended up working better than anything he could have envisioned. It's not that hard to explain away."

Raptor was unconvinced. "But if Hawkins was working *with* Steven, then how come Steven's dead? That doesn't make any sense."

Charon swore again loudly as he slammed his hand on the table, the resulting vibration sending the empty glass crashing to the floor, where it broke into several large pieces. "I can't believe your still defending him! You still seem to have this. . .unrealistic perception of the man and are blind to how he manipulated you!"

Walking over to the bed, Charon laid back down and shifted around until he was comfortable. "I'm done with this conversation. You're like a brother, but you can be really stupid sometimes. If you want to help these guys, then you can do it without me. I'm done. Good night."

Raptor wanted to say more, but knew from past experience that he would likely have more success convincing a *Pandora's Box* addict to give away a free session than he would reasoning with Charon. His mind was made up, and now Raptor had an even tougher decision to make.

Knowing that sleep would be impossible now, he got up from the bed, grabbed his *svith-scale* jacket from the back of the chair and left the room.

Chapter 20

Contrasting Worldviews

*A*fter leaving the hotel room, Raptor took an elevator down
to the main lobby area. Turning to his left, he entered the
bar and grill, which never closed. The Vagabond Hotel served
mostly middle class clientele, and, being located on the eastern
edge of Elysium, they consisted largely of travelers who were
entering or exiting the large city. However, in addition to the
legitimate crowd, the owners of the establishment also had
dealings with several, well-established criminal organizations.
Underneath the hotel, there were hidden tunnels that were
often used by smugglers and contraband dealers that wished
to avoid the customs inspectors at the main gates to the city.
As such, there was always a contingent of colorful characters
milling about the hotel at any given moment.

As Raptor entered the area, he immediately recognized
several drug runners seated at the bar, their boisterous laughter
momentarily drowning out the ambient sounds of the various
holo-projectors showing highlights from the recent sporting
events. Due to the nature of his underhanded business dealings, Raptor had long ago trained himself to casually study
his surroundings upon entering any room. In addition to the
raucous group at the bar, there were several other smaller
groups of patrons huddled together in the booths, as well as a

smattering of what looked to be romantic couples enjoying a night out. The only person of interest in the whole place was a man sitting alone in a booth near the back of the room, a grey fedora casting shadows over his face and making it impossible to see his features. Recognizing the hat as belonging to Gunther, Raptor made his way over to the booth. As he neared the table, he saw the man's head lift just enough for his eyes to observe who it was that approached. To Raptor's surprise, the face under the hat did not belong to the old man.

"What do you want?" Braedon said in disdain, clearly wanting to be left alone. The man's abrasive attitude grated on Raptor's irritated nerves. Nevertheless, Raptor slid down into the bench opposite the soldier. Braedon lowered his head once more and stared at the half-empty glass of soda in front of him as Raptor calmly ordered a drink from the holographic menu mounted against the wall. Once he had finished, Braedon tried again.

"In case you didn't notice, I don't really feel like company right now."

Raptor leaned forward, his arms resting on the table. "Don't you think it's a little unwise for you to be out in public? Your face is still being plastered all over the holofeeds. Some of the people in here wouldn't hesitate for a second to turn you in."

"I'm not some rookie," Braedon shot back. "I know the risks. And I also know how to keep my face hidden. Why do you think I took Gunther's hat and coat?"

"That may be true, but you're drawing attention to yourself by sitting alone in the corner," Raptor stated as he sat back. "There are many who would take quick advantage of a loner. I don't think even your quick reflexes would save you."

"So, what do you want?" Braedon grumbled. "Do you need something, or did you just come down here to lecture me?"

"Actually, I didn't even know you were down here. I came to get a drink myself."

Shrugging, Braedon took a sip of his soda. "So, have you and the others decided what to do about Gunther and I? Are you going to help us, or turn us in?"

Raptor smiled. He didn't much like the soldier, but he at least admired his brazenness. "Jade and Xavier both want to help, each for their own reasons. And, although this may come as a surprise to you," he said sarcastically, "Charon thinks we should go for the reward money."

"And what have *you* decided?" Braedon asked.

"Honestly, I want to turn you in also and be done with it," Raptor said nonchalantly, as if the topic of conversation simply revolved around what dessert to have. "But, that would be the easy way out, at least temporarily. The good news is for you, I don't mind choosing the hard road if I think it's in my best interest."

"And you're convinced that helping us *is* in your best interest?"

"Yes, I do," Raptor replied. "I'm convinced by the data that the old man collected that Mathison's planning on turning all of us into unthinking robots. And frankly, I've kind of grown attached to my free will."

At that moment, the two men paused in their conversation as a waitress brought Raptor the drink he had ordered. Once she was out of earshot, Raptor continued. "So, I guess for the time being, Xavier, Jade and I will be accompanying you on this little errand."

Secretly relieved that Charon would not be coming along but not wanting to reveal that to the man's best friend, Braedon finished his soda and ordered another one before replying. "On behalf of Gunther and I, we're grateful for your help," he said sincerely. "And. . .I'm sorry if I've come across as. . .harsh. It's just that. . .it's been a tough day for me. I hope you can understand that Steven was more than just my teacher. He was my friend and. . .and the closest thing I've had to a father since coming to Elysium."

Raptor was surprised at the twinge of emotions sparked by Braedon's words. The fact that they echoed his own recent sentiments struck a chord in his inner being. "I *do* understand. I don't know if you knew this, but I was also trained by Steven. He was my teacher for six years when I was a young man."

"I wondered about that," Braedon said. "I noticed a similarity in the way you moved and attacked that Guardian. You reflect Steven's style."

"So I take it that Steven had something to do with you getting involved in Crimson Liberty," Raptor commented.

Braedon nodded. "When I first came through the portal, I went through the normal emotional issues that just about everyone faces. During the initial arrival interview, I mentioned that I was in the military back on Earth. The Transition Counselor hooked me up with Steven."

"Did you. . .have any family back on Earth?" Raptor asked, an odd tone to his voice.

"Yes, a wife," Braedon said with sudden emotion. "If it hadn't been for Steven's friendship, I don't think I would have made it. He took me under his wing, taught me, helped me get over the emotional pain of being separated from my wife by introducing me to Jesus."

After a short pause, Raptor broke the uncomfortable silence with a chuckle. "You make it sound like Jesus is a personal friend or something."

"He is," Braedon said without hesitation. With the grief over losing Steven still so fresh, he didn't feel like sharing any more about his personal journey to faith with this murderer and thief. Yet, he also knew that there would be no greater way to honor the memory of his mentor than to tell this man about the very thing that had been most important to him.

"So I take it you don't believe in the Celestials?" Raptor said, diverting the topic somewhat.

"No, I don't," Braedon replied.

"Why not?" Raptor asked in genuine curiosity.

"Because there's no evidence for it," Braedon answered.

"But, you believe in a *God* you can't see," Raptor countered. "Where's the evidence for that?"

Braedon paused for a moment to collect his thoughts and to offer a quick prayer for guidance. *God, why this? Why now? Can't I just grieve in peace? I don't know if I can even think clearly, much less try to defend my belief in you to this criminal.* Despite his reticence, he remembered Steven's last request and felt the clear confirmation in his heart that he should continue. Taking a deep breath, he let it out slowly. "Are you sure you want to hear my answer? This is a pretty deep topic."

"Bring it on," Raptor stated. "It's not like we're in a hurry at the moment."

"Fine. Then let me answer your question with another question: have you ever seen Earth?"

"No," Raptor stated.

"So then, how do you know it even exists?"

"Wait a second. This is a totally different situation," Raptor protested. "There have been thousands of people who have come from there, including yourself, and they bring with them pictures, music, videos and all sorts of evidence proving that it exists."

"Granted. But still, you've never seen it yourself, have you."

"Okay, no, I haven't," Raptor admitted.

"And I would argue that it *isn't* different with the existence of God," Braedon said. "In fact, let me take this back even one more step: how do you know that *anything* is real, or true?"

"You go with what your senses tell you and you use logical deduction," Raptor replied, having thought through this issue since reading Steven's journal.

"Right. Whether we realize consciously or not, we all make constant judgments about things we encounter or hear to decide if they are true or false," Braedon stated. "If we don't let our emotions get in the way and we think clearly, we do this much the same way a scientist would perform an experiment: we gather information, examine the data, and draw a conclusion.

"Let me explain it another way," Braedon continued. "Why have you decided to risk your life to help Gunther and I?"

Raptor shrugged. "Because I'm convinced that it's in my best interest to do so."

"Okay. And how were you convinced of this?"

Raptor paused. "Mostly by the governmental documents that were taken from the Research and Records building."

"But how do you know that those weren't falsified?" Braedon asked.

"Because I've seen enough real ones in my time to know a fake when I see it," Raptor answered. "These have all of the markings of being legit."

"And what about Gunther?" Braedon pressed on. "He claims to be able to open the portals back to earth. Do you believe him? How do you even know if he's really a scientist?"

"Because I did a little background check on the two of you," Raptor remarked bluntly. "And, frankly, Gunther looks and *acts* like a scientist and *you* look and act like a soldier."

"Fair enough. But how do you know we aren't spies?"

"Because no one is foolish enough to allow one of their friends to get killed in order to gain the trust of the enemy," Raptor said, bringing back once again a reminder of Steven's sacrifice. "It doesn't make any logical sense. I saw the surprise on Gunther's face when he pulled the trigger on the Vortex. His reaction was genuine. And, you and Steven risked your own necks to help what you thought was *Box*-addicted nutcase. No. You're not spies."

"So what you're saying is that you're convinced of the *reliability* of the government documents, you trust the *authority* of the information you received from the background checks, those two things match what your *experience* tells you, and your *logic* confirms it. Right?" Braedon reiterated.

"Yeah. So what's your point?" Raptor asked.

"The point is that this is the same process we use to determine if a worldview, or religion, is true or not. Each worldview attempts to answer four basic questions," Braedon continued. "The answers to those questions form the basic beliefs of that worldview. Once you know those basic beliefs, you can put them through the 'truth-filter' that we just discussed to determine if they meet all of those criteria of reliability, authority, etc."

Raptor was silent for a second as he analyzed every word in Braedon's statement. "I suppose the questions that form one's worldview have to do with what we believe about religion and the existence of God."

"Yes and no. A worldview is more broad then that," Braedon explained. "The four basic questions are: 1) Where did we come from? – Origin. 2) Why is there pain and suffering? – Evil. 3) What's the purpose of life? – Meaning. 4) What's going to happen to us when we die? – Destiny."

Caught up in the discussion, Braedon began to forget his grief and his countenance brightened up as he became more animated. "When we search deep enough, we'll find that we *all* have a basic set of beliefs that help us make sense of the world around us. These beliefs then form the foundation on which all the decisions in our daily life are based. Unfortunately, most people don't even realize they *have* a worldview, much less think through the logic behind it. Let me give you an example. You believe in evolution, right?"

"Yeah. Don't most intelligent people?" Raptor asked, deliberately trying to goad on his companion.

Braedon just ignored the jibe. "Okay. Correct me if I'm wrong, but the way you would answer the basic worldview questions would be as follows.

"Question one: Where did we come from? In the beginning there was nothing, then it exploded in the Big Bang. Over billions of years, the material from the explosion formed the stars, then planets. Eventually the earth cooled and water formed. Chemicals mixed together and were struck by lightning, which created the first single-celled organism. Then, over millions of years, that organism evolved higher and higher until it became modern humans. Then, humans were transported here to Tartarus about two hundred years ago. Is that an accurate summary?"

Raptor grimaced. "I guess that's pretty close. But the way you put it, it doesn't sound nearly so scientific. I'm sure a scientist wouldn't explain it as 'nothing exploded' to create everything."

"Have you ever read any scientific material explaining the origin of the universe?" Braedon countered.

"Not really, but I know some very smart people who have, and I trust their opinion," Raptor said.

"So you're trusting someone else's authority. Hold that thought, because I'll come back to it," Braedon said. "Question two: Why is there so much suffering? Well, if evolution is *true* and we evolved from animals over millions of years through survival of the fittest, then the problem of why there's suffering in the world isn't a problem at all. There's suffering because it's just the way things are. It's part of evolution. Right?"

"That's right," Raptor said. "I've experienced 'survival of the fittest' firsthand when I was growing up on the streets as a teen."

"But have you ever considered the ramifications of this idea?" Braedon asked. "If we are all just glorified animals, then there's no such thing as morality. There *is* no right or wrong."

"Right," Raptor confirmed. "I'm not accountable to anyone but myself."

"So if someone were to rob you, or kill your wife or parents, would you just throw your hands up and just say, 'Oh well. That's life. Or would something within you want to cry out for justice?"

Braedon knew that something he'd said struck a nerve as Raptor's face changed rapidly and became somber and serious.

When he didn't reply to the question, Braedon continued, choosing his words carefully.

"Let's move on to question three: What's the purpose of life? How do we fix all of the suffering? If evolution is your worldview, then everyone should live however they please. The best we can hope for to eliminate suffering of people is a man-made utopia, which is exactly what Mathison is striving for. He's actually being very consistent with his own worldview. With that said, do you believe Mathison is wrong in trying to control everyone?"

Raptor could see the logical trap he had fallen into, but knew he couldn't get out of it. "I guess, *based on my worldview*, that I'd have to say no, because there's no such thing as right and wrong," he said in defeat. "But, I think you could make an argument that, because he is infringing on the free will of others, he's wrong."

"But who decided that 'infringing on the will of others' is wrong? You?"

Raptor let out a chuckle. "That's *my* opinion, and the opinion of many others."

"Are you saying, then, that if a majority believes something, that makes it moral?" Braedon asked, doing his best to keep his tone neutral so as not to offend his companion.

"No, but the majority will have the power to *enforce* their opinion," Raptor replied, becoming slightly frustrated.

"Alright, I don't want to belabor the point," Braedon said. "Last question: what will happen to us when we die?"

Grabbing his glass, Raptor took a long drink of the liquid. As he did so, Braedon noticed that his hand seemed to shake slightly, as if the topic of conversation had caused a sudden, unexpected fear in his companion. "According to evolution," Braedon stated, "the answer to this question is simple: nothing. If all that exists is mere matter, then when a person dies, they simply cease to exist. There is no afterlife. No heaven and no hell. As you said, there's no one to hold each of us accountable.

"The consequence of this idea is that, since this life is all there is, we should get as much pleasure as we can and reduce the amount of pain. In other words, we should live each day for our own pleasure. 'Eat, drink, and be merry, for tomorrow we die.'"

"That's a pretty good motto," Raptor said smugly. "I'll have to remember that one."

"Nice," Braedon commented dryly. "The problem with that worldview is that it's bad for society. Children, elderly, the handicapped and other defenseless people suffer."

"That's too bad for them," Raptor said casually.

"I'm sure you'd feel different if you were in their shoes," Braedon said, his patience starting to ebb from the man's callousness. "We're all just one accident away from being handicapped. If that shot from the police officer had hit you just a few inches from your shoulder, you could have been permanently crippled."

At the mention of the wound, Raptor could feel it throb anew. Reaching down, he grabbed his glass and took another drink to dull the sudden pain. "Okay, so you've explained my worldview pretty good. Now explain yours."

Taking a drink of his own, Braedon considered his words carefully before speaking. "Origin – God created the universe, including Earth. He created all of the animals and plants with amazing capabilities, but his special creation was mankind. We are so special, in fact, that he made us in his image. This sets us apart from the rest of the animals."

"I take it that's why most of you Christians are hung up on fighting against abortion and euthanasia, and you make such a big deal about the rights of the infirm."

"Exactly. In fact, the very concept that 'all men are created equal' is only possible with a Christian worldview," Braedon stated. "After all, it's kind of hard to be *created* equal without a Creator."

"Yeah, well that's probably why I never bought into that idea. So how do you answer the second question about suffering?" Raptor asked. "If God is such a good God, then why do people suffer?"

"Well, the complete answer to that question would require a lot more time to answer," Braedon replied. "The short version is that God didn't want to create a bunch of puppets that would worship him because they were programmed that way. He gave humans free will. We chose to rebel against him, and the universe has been suffering ever since. In fact, Christianity is the only worldview that can adequately explain why there is such goodness and beauty in the world, but also such horror and evil. Furthermore, we have a firm foundation for morals and ethics. Since God created the world, he decides what is right and wrong. He sets the standards based on his character. We compare everything else to his perfection."

"Making you into self-righteous hypocrites in the process," Raptor said snidely.

Taking a deep breath, Braedon fought against his natural inclinations to retaliate verbally. "I disagree. If you understood Christianity better, you might realize that because we believe that 'all have sinned and have fallen short of the glory of God', then we believe that we are no better than anyone else. We are beggars telling other beggars where to find food. Our self-esteem is not based on our own goodness, but on Christ's sacrifice. Our worth is based solely on the fact that God loves us."

"If you say so," Raptor quipped. "So how do Christians think we should live? Should we all give away our money to the poor and follow lists of 'do's and don'ts'?"

"Christians simply believe that since God is our creator, he knows how we should act to get the most out of life. He wrote our 'instruction manual' and if we follow his guidelines, we can live life to its fullest. He didn't write the Bible and the laws to ruin our fun, but to show us the right path. We believe that there are *moral* laws just as there are *physical* laws. We can *say* we don't believe in gravity, but we still face the consequences if we chose to go against it. In the same way, people can *say* they don't believe in moral laws, but if they chose to ignore them, they'll still be forced to pay the consequences."

"Like what?" Raptor asked.

"Take sex, for example," Braedon said. "God designed sex to be a beautiful way for a husband and wife to express their love for each other, and as a way to produce children. But mankind has chosen to ignore God's design and use sex merely for their own selfish pleasure. And by doing so, they have to pay the consequences, such as disease, emotional pain, unwanted pregnancy, etc."

Raptor looked impressed. "I have to say I've never heard that explanation from any religious person. Then again, I don't really know very many 'religious people' – especially not Christians – and I certainly don't make it a habit of having deep philosophical conversations with them. In fact, I usually try to avoid topics revolving around religion or politics."

Braedon grinned at his comment. "I'm not surprised. Unfortunately, those are the two most important topics you can discuss. Anyway, ultimately, God sums up the question of how we should live by simply saying that we should love him with all of our hearts and love our neighbors as ourselves," Braedon stated.

"Which includes giving away your money and following lists of 'do's and don'ts'," Raptor reiterated.

Braedon sighed in frustration. "You're missing the point. It's not about what we *do*. We are forgiven because of Christ's sacrifice. We do good in *response* to his love, not in order to *earn* it."

"Whatever," Raptor said. "I'm guessing your answer to the fourth question is that when you die, 'true believers' will live forever in paradise, while the heathen masses burn forever in hell. Don't you think that's a little harsh?"

"Listen, Raptor," Braedon said, "I'm just trying to give an overview of the beliefs of Christianity. If you've got a few months, I'd be happy to answer all of your various questions."

Raptor's jovial mood vanished instantly at Braedon's words, making him review what he had said in order to figure out what might have offended him.

"Yeah, well, I'm really not interested in learning more about your religion," Raptor said abruptly.

Braedon frowned. "Then why the interest? Why were you asking me all these questions, then?"

Shrugging, Raptor took another drink from his glass. "For conversation's sake, I guess. I'm not really interested in any religion, especially not one whose adherents think that they have a specific corner on the truth. I don't want to end up as a close-minded hypocrite."

Half-a-dozen verbal retaliations came instantly to Braedon's mind. However, he knew that any one of them would only reinforce Raptor's distorted image of Christians and their beliefs. Breathing deeply to calm his emotions, Braedon finally responded. "Let me ask you one more thing: how do you define 'close-minded'?"

Raptor paused, caught off guard by the unexpected question and simultaneously impressed that the soldier was able to keep his temper under control despite the blatant insults to his faith. Although he was growing somewhat weary of the conversation, he had to admit that he liked the way the man thought. His questions were interesting and surprisingly well thought-out. *Steven has obviously trained him well,* he mused. "Basically, it's what I already said: someone who is close-minded is someone who thinks their beliefs are true and everyone else's are false. They close their minds off to other ideas and evidence."

"Okay, then let me ask you something," Braedon said. "If you were going to have surgery, would you want a close-minded surgeon? Would you want a surgeon who had studied and knew the truth about the body, or one who was 'open-minded' to other alternative methods that had been scientifically proven to be false? Or, if you were on trial, would you want a lawyer that stood up in court and said, 'Ladies and Gentlemen of the jury, I ask you to be open-minded about my client. Don't listen to what the eyewitnesses say and don't examine the evidence, just be open to these other theories about what happened that night.'"

"Nice try, but that analogy doesn't hold up," Raptor commented. "It's not the same. You're saying that there's absolute truth, right? I read something that Steven wrote about the subject. But the problem with your analogy is that religion is not something that can be proven scientifically. It's all about arbitrary beliefs that can't be demonstrated to be true or false."

At the mention of his departed mentor's name, a shadow passed over Braedon as his grief, which had been momentarily forgotten, came rushing back upon him. Offering up a quick prayer for strength, Braedon replied. "I'll admit that no worldview can be 'scientifically proven', but I *would* argue that the Christian worldview *can* be shown to be true in other ways."

"Really?" Raptor said skeptically. "How?"

"Much the same way a jury can decide if a person is guilty or innocent," Braedon replied. "Look, because a crime happens at a specific point in time, it can't be 'proven' in the same way that a scientific experiment can prove something because a scientific experiment is repeatable and observable. The best a prosecuting attorney can do is demonstrate that the eyewitness reports and evidence *support* one conclusion. The jury then decides if the evidence is *strong enough* to convict the defendant."

"Wait a second," Raptor said, holding up a hand for emphasis. "Are you insinuating that we should do the same with religion? But what eyewitnesses can you interview? What evidence is there for a belief system? That just doesn't make sense."

"But there *is* evidence," Braedon countered. "Every religion, every worldview makes claims about reality. Therefore, I believe it's the job of every thinking person to use logic and reasoning to examine the claims of a worldview to decide if it aligns with what is real. Is the worldview consistent, or does it contradict itself? Is it comprehensive, or does it leave some important questions unanswered? Does it match what we see in reality?

"One should also look at the history of how the belief system came to be formed," Braedon continued earnestly. "When you think about it, these ancient texts are really like eyewitness reports. So we need to ask ourselves questions about them. Who wrote them? When were they written? Are they consistent within themselves? Do they match what we know about the culture and time during which they were written? Did the founder have any ulterior motives? You said that you trust what scientists say about the origin of life. Why? Because you respect their authority. The same holds true with ancient documents. If they are shown to be reliable through archaeology and other sources, then this increases their authority in general. To sum it up, you need to ask, 'who says?' and 'by what authority?'."

"Alright, you can stop now. I get your point," Raptor said. "However, none of this really answers my first question: how can you prove the existence of a God you can't see?"

Braedon answered without hesitation. "But it *does* answer the question. If you study all of the great belief systems – Hinduism, Buddhism, Christianity, Islam, Judaism, Athiesm, etc – you will see that they are all trying to explain reality. They are worldviews that attempt to answer the big questions of life. I believe that if you judge each of them based on their truth claims, you'll realize that only Christianity makes sense of all of the evidence. Only Christianity is internally consistent. And only Christianity ultimately makes logical sense. Thus, it proves that God exists."

A smug look plastered itself on Raptor's face. "Those are some pretty weighty claims."

"The bottom line, Raptor, is that whatever worldview we decide is the truth will ultimately determine the course of our life by creating the foundation upon which all other decisions are made," Braedon stated. "Most importantly, we need to answer the question of what will happen to us when we die, for the answer to that question will tell us how we should live."

Finishing the last swig of his drink, Raptor placed his thumb on the reader to pay his bill, then stood up. "I appreciate the 'five-point lecture', and I'm mildly impressed to find that you've thought this out. However, I'm really not interested in researching what different religions teach, since I don't believe in God at all. Besides, you may have noticed that I'm not exactly in a position to do an intense net-search right now."

Sensing the other's desire to end the conversation, Braedon quickly offered his last point. "Believe me, I understand. However, I would encourage you not to brush it off. Would you be willing to bet your soul that you're right? Are you really *that* convinced that there is no God? If I were you, I'd make it more of a priority, *especially* considering our current predicament. After all, none of us knows the day or the hour that we'll die."

Raptor stiffened. Unnerved by Braedon's words, he forced himself to offer his companion a final, unnatural grin. "Thanks. I'll keep that in mind. I suggest you get some rest. We're going to have a long ride ahead of us tomorrow."

Turning quickly to indicate that the conversation was over, Raptor walked briskly toward the exit. Not wanting to return to his room, he chose to go outside for a walk to clear his head. He'd come downstairs to the bar seeking to forget his nightmare, yet the questions and arguments that Braedon raised only served to create within his tortured mind a different kind of nightmare – one that pursued him relentlessly as he left the hotel and strode down the mostly empty streets of Elysium.

Chapter 21

Leaving the City

*G*unther stared out the window of the Cliffjumper as it glided along quietly in the tunnel. He was so enveloped with his own thoughts and memories that he was completely oblivious to the conversation that was being held in the front of the truck. Since the heavy-duty, utility vehicle could fit up to eight passengers, the six of them had room to spare, even considering their supplies and equipment. Charon, who had changed his mind about coming with them, drove, while Raptor sat in the passenger seat, Jade and Xavier were in the middle, and Braedon and Gunther were in the rear seats. For a moment, Gunther glanced over at the soldier sitting next to him, wondering if he too felt like a prisoner. Although Raptor and his co-conspirators had offered to help try to open the portals back to Earth, Gunther wondered if there wasn't some ulterior motive.

Looking back out the window, Gunther pulled up the cowl of his gray trench coat to ward off an imagined chill that ran through his body. He fingered his fedora that sat in his lap as he thought back on all that had transpired. Although only five years had passed since he had arrived in Elysium, his time before entering the portal now seemed like nothing more than a wonderful dream. Even the faces of his beloved wife,

Eveleen, and his nephew, Erik, had begun to fade with the passage of time. His stomach cramped tightly from the emotions that suddenly overwhelmed him at the memory of his loved ones. Erik was lost to him forever, but perhaps, just maybe, if this journey was successful, he could hold his wife once again.

The tiny sliver of hope that he treasured in his heart was constantly under assault by numerous, pessimistic thoughts about what obstacles might still lie in his path. *Will we be able to make it to Dehali, or will we get caught before we get there? Will Raptor and his companions eventually betray Braedon and I? Did Travis make it to Dehali? Will I be able to find him? Will I be able to get the Vortex to open the portals? When will the war start?*

"We're approaching the end of the tunnel," Charon's voice announced. "In another minute, we should make it to the edge of the main road leaving 'that shining jewel known as, Elysium.'"

Charon's words served to drive away the disturbing thoughts plaguing Gunther, for the time being. Brought back to the present, he scowled at the man driving the vehicle. Early this morning at the hotel, when Braedon first mentioned that the big brute had decided *not* to join them, Gunther had felt intense relief and elation. But it proved to be short lived. As their small group was preparing to leave, Charon approached Raptor and informed him that he had decided to come after all, much to the disappointment of Gunther and Braedon. The man's hostility toward the two outsiders was palpable, and his presence only served to heighten Gunther's already elevated stress levels.

The hovering vehicle in which he rode began to slow down as it approached the end of the tunnel. Charon kept the truck at a slow crawl as Raptor transmitted the proper code to the door. Even though Gunther was uncomfortable in the company of these criminals, he was nevertheless grateful for their assistance. Had he and Braedon been on their own, he wondered how they could have possibly escaped the city undetected. But for Raptor and his friends, this was an everyday occurrence. From what Gunther could gather from snippets of conversation, there were several of these access tunnels leading into and out of Elysium, all of which were kept secret from the general public. Few people even knew they existed, and only those with the right connections could actually use them.

"All clear," Raptor said. Charon immediately hit the accelerator and drove the Cliffjumper out of the tunnel. Gunther's eyes widened as the vehicle turned a corner and passed between two rocky outcroppings and merged onto the main road. Looking out the window on the left side of the vehicle, Gunther could see the entire city.

The Globe was just rising in the east, spreading its early morning light throughout the entire gigantic cavern. The shining, purple walls of the underground world seemed alive as they reflected the rays from the man-made device. The road on which the group now traveled reached toward the eastern wall, and behind them, Gunther could see that it headed west for several miles before turning north to cross the magnificent Elysium bridge. Flowing beneath the shining, golden structure, ran a wide, silvery river that seemed to sparkle and glisten with color and light. The river ran parallel to the road until finally passing under another bridge as it neared the eastern wall.

"I take it you've never seen the city from out here," Braedon said, which were the first words he'd spoken since they had departed from the hotel. "It's quite a sight, huh?"

Gunther simply nodded, still in awe at the beauty that stretched out before him. After several more seconds of admiring the view, he turned to face Braedon. "I've always felt like Elysium was a prison. I've tried for so long to find a way out, I never stopped to consider its full beauty."

"That's a common feeling," Braedon replied, "especially amongst 1st Geners. According to the historians, that's why there's been so much debate over the names of places. Did you ever see the holovid about the naming of Tartarus?"

"No," Gunther said curiously. "I remember the people in the Welcome Center told me something about it when I first arrived, but I was in so much shock I didn't really retain anything."

"They say that the First Colony spent their entire lives trying to get back to Earth," Braedon began. "Like you, they felt that this place was a prison, so they named it 'Tartarus', after the prison of the underworld in classic mythology. They also called the river 'Styx', which was the river that supposedly led the dead to the underworld. To them, this place was like a type of hell: a place of torment.

"However, their children, who had been born and raised in Tartarus, decided to give up searching for a way back to Earth and chose to build a life here," Braedon continued. "Fights and skirmishes would often break out between those still arriving from Earth through the portals and the 2nd Geners. Over the years, those who were native to Tartarus began to resent the idea that their home was a prison and wanted to change the names. But by that time, the names of Tartarus and Styx had become ingrained in the culture. But when the city was built by the native-borns, they wanted a positive name that would reflect its beauty and majesty."

Gunther let out a loud 'harumph'. "So they settled on Elysium, the name for 'paradise' or 'heaven' in mythology. I'd always wondered why there was such a contrast between the names. How interesting. I have to admit, the purple coloring in the rock is quite marvelous. And the way the fish and other creatures in the river produce their own colorful biolumines-cence is spectacular." Gunther paused suddenly, his expression becoming serious. "Tell me honestly, Braedon. Do you think we have any chance of succeeding? And do you really think that Raptor and his crew are going to help us, or do they have something else more sinister in mind?"

Braedon stared at the older man for a moment before answering. "I've been living in Tartarus now for ten years. After all that time, I had given up hope on ever seeing my wife again. Then, just when I'd finally come to grips with that reality, you show up. I know you don't believe in God, but I have to tell you that *I'm* convinced that I'm following the path that he has laid before me. I don't know what lies at the end of that path, but I can tell you this: He is with us."

Gunther tried to smile, but it wilted into a grimace. "You know, there truly are times I wish I believed in God. I wish I could believe that there is a purpose to life – a 'path' that is being laid out by an intelligence that has my best interest in mind. Unfortunately, I don't believe," he finished, matter-of-factly. Turning to look out the window once again, Gunther stared at the city that had been his home for the past five years. "No. I don't believe. . ."

Epilogue

*T*aj El-Mofty stared at the beautifully crafted mosaic that adorned the wall of the Imam's private room. Although he'd been here numerous times, the way in which the artist had woven the calligraphy reciting a text of the Qur'an into the geometric shapes never ceased to capture his attention.

The door to the room suddenly opened, drawing Taj's attention away from the mosaic. His heart leapt into his throat in excitement as the holy man he had been waiting for stepped inside. The Imam was dressed in an embroidered, solid gray *kurta* shirt with matching pants. Adorning his head was a traditional, white *taqiyah* hat rimmed with gold that contrasted sharply with his dark, full beard and mustache. Before the door had even closed completely, Taj crossed over to the man, the news he had to share nearly bursting from within him.

"Asalaam Alaykum," Taj said in greeting as he shook the Imam's right hand.

"Alaykum Asalaam," the Imam said in return. As he spoke, the Imam walked over to one of the two red-gold couches that filled the center of the room and sat down. "What news do you bring that is so important that you had to see me so quickly after the noon prayers?"

Taj took a deep breath to calm himself. "Ya Mu'aleem, we just received word from our informant in Elysium that a scientist and former government guard have stolen a secret weapon from Mathison's research facility."

The Imam's right eyebrow rose at the report. "What kind of weapon?"

"He said that he didn't know. But, he believes, based on his source, that the weapon can produce great power, and also might be used to stabilize the portals, thus opening the way back to earth!"

"And where is this scientist now?"

"He is headed toward Dehali to meet up with a colleague," Taj continued.

The Imam stood quickly to his feet and began pacing the room, speaking his thoughts aloud. "We must have this weapon. This is the sign we have been waiting for. The men are ready, our plans are in place, and now. . .this gift!" Turning, he stared at Taj, who was now also standing. "I want you to take some men to Dehali and find this scientist. We need to discover what this weapon can do, and if it can indeed open the doorway back to Earth. Then. . .we will wipe out the infidels here in Jaheem and return to Earth triumphant! Perhaps the presence of our army and technology on Earth will usher in the reign of the Twelfth Imam!"

"Imam Ahmed, there is one more bit of information that will be of great interest to you," Taj El-Mofty said, his voice laced with adrenaline.

The Islamic leader turned to face his general, his expression one of intense curiosity. "Yes?"

"We have learned that the scientist and his soldier friend are being aided by a criminal and his companions," Taj reported.

The Imam frowned. "And why is this of interest?"

"Because the criminal's code name is Raptor," Taj announced. "But his real name is Rahib Ahmed. Your son!"

Afterword

*A*t some point in each of our lives, we have to ask ourselves, "What do I believe?" and "Why do I believe it?" Often, the first question is fairly easy to answer. We have certain beliefs that we've gathered over time, almost as if through osmosis. But the second question is much harder to answer. Why do we believe what we believe? Most people, if they are honest, will answer, "Because that's what I was taught."

But is that really a good answer? What if we were taught wrong? What if our 'teacher', usually our parents, was wrong? If so, how do we know what is right? By what criteria do we determine the truth of something?

Every day we hear news stories, co-workers and friends tell us about things that happened to them, we receive e-mails from people that give us information, etc. In each of these cases, we have to decide if we are going to believe what we read, or are told. But how do we decide? We do it in much the same way a jury would decide the guilt or innocence of the accused in a court case, albeit in a much less formal setting.

Arguably the biggest factor is the source. If the source is a friend or family member, we almost instantly believe the story. But what happens if the trustworthiness of the source is in question? In that case, we have to do a bit more digging. In addition to seeking out evidence for the reliability of the person, we would also need to ask other questions, such as the ones that Braedon brought up in Chapter 20: Does the story make sense? Is the story internally consistent? Does the source have a motive for lying? Do other witnesses or evidence corroborate the story?

As you may have already guessed, the other three books in *The Tartarus Chronicles* will deal with each of these questions as they pertain to belief systems, religions, and worldviews. For the purpose of this Afterword, I want to go in another direction.

To even have a rational debate on the issue of what is true, you have to first pre-suppose that there is a truth worth pursuing. In other words, truth has to be absolute. It cannot be relative.

In past decades, speakers could give presentations and debates to audiences who would challenge the beliefs of the presenter. But in recent times, audiences will sit attentively and listen to a presenter, clap politely when he/she is finished, and leave quietly at the end. The reason for this change is that our young people today are being taught that all truth is relative. "What is true for you may not be true for me." With that mindset, there is no reason to debate anything.

As an example, this issue is often seen when people use the word, "tolerance". According to the Online Oxford Dictionary, the word "tolerant" is defined as "showing willingness to allow the existence of opinions or behavior that one does not necessarily agree with." However, many alter this definition slightly to mean more than just "willingness to allow the existence of opinions or behaviors", but also to mean "acceptance" of those opinions or behaviors as equal to one's own. The difference is subtle, but has enormous implications.

For example, let's say I have a friend who is a Hindu. I may believe that Hinduism is not the truth, but he's still my friend and I treat him with respect. If given an opportunity, I would try to have a conversation about my beliefs in order to try to win him over to my way of thinking, since I believe it to be the truth. Therefore, I am being tolerant in the original sense.

However, under the new definition of tolerance, I would have to also say that his beliefs are as equally valid and "true" as my own Christian beliefs. If I were to claim that his beliefs are wrong and my beliefs are correct, then I would be labeled as "intolerant." But consider carefully the worldview that underlies that definition: all religions are man-made belief systems, and as such, none of them are ultimately true or false. All are equal.

But what is really at stake is the very idea of truth itself. In this example, Christianity and Hinduism are making contrasting claims about what is true. So the new definition of "intolerance" is like stating that I'm a bigot because my belief that gravity prevents a person from flying is offensive to those who want to fly! In the same way, a person might call me a bigot because I believe that accepting the free gift of salvation offered by Jesus is the only way to salvation. However, just because a belief might be "disagreeable" to someone doesn't mean it isn't true. It's truth or falsehood should be determined by analyzing it's claims, not by observing the feelings it evokes in someone.

Unfortunately, many people don't realize this error. Instead, they let their feelings take over and, without offering logical reasoning for why they believe a certain worldview to be true or false, they resort to name-calling. Rather than coming up with a calm, well thought-out argument to prove a point, they use inflammatory terms. One example of this is that recent authors have claimed that to teach a child about religion is akin to child abuse. This is not a reasoned argument proving the truth or falsehood of Christianity. Instead, it serves to bring forth feelings of injustice in many people.

Another common phrase that is used in regards to "tolerance" is: "You shouldn't force your beliefs on others." However, when you consider this statement carefully, you will see that it is self-refuting. The person making the statement is doing the very thing he/she states shouldn't be done! If people truly believed that it was wrong to impose beliefs on other people, then they wouldn't impose their own beliefs on you by telling you not to impose your beliefs!

It is a sad reality that many people don't seek answers to the big questions in life until it is too late. They go through life with a belief system that, if examined closely, would reveal glaring inconsistencies. Take for example the moral atheist. In recent years, atheist groups have placed billboards in various cities at Christmas time with slogans such as, "Be good for goodness sake," or "You can be good without God." However, these slogans are making an important, yet common, mistake: the question is not whether one *can* be good apart from God, but rather *on what basis* should one be good apart from God? An atheist has no logical ground for acting in a moral way, since, in his/her eyes, there is no lawgiver.

Let me give you an example made popular by writer Frank Peretti. Imagine a school playground teeming with children. They are, for the most part, playing well with each other and sharing the equipment: balls, jump ropes, etc. Why? Because the teacher is standing there and watching everything the kids are doing and making sure they follow the "Playground Rules", which are posted on a big sign on the wall. In addition, the teacher will discipline any students who break the rules by making them stand against the wall, thus losing playtime.

But what would happen if, one day, the teacher wasn't there? For a while, the kids would probably play as they always had. But then, when it comes time for little Jimmy to give the ball up so another child can play with it, Jimmy decides that he wants to keep it. The other kids yell, "That's not fair! You've got to follow the rules!" To which Jimmy replies, "Who says? Are you gonna make me?"

When the other kids see that Jimmy didn't follow the rules and didn't face any consequences, the playground atmosphere deteriorates quickly. Before long, everyone is pushing, shoving, taking things from each other, etc. And who rules the playground? The biggest, meanest kid. Thus you have "survival of the fittest".

In the same way, when God is removed from the picture, then there is no longer a moral absolute with which to measure behavior. Atheists may still be moral people, but they no longer have the *authority* upon which to base that morality. It becomes completely subjective. They must live inconsistent with their beliefs.

On the flip side, Christians act inconsistent with their beliefs when they *don't* love their neighbors. There are many Christians who violate the teachings of Jesus and sin in numerous ways, and many later ask for forgiveness for doing so. It's not a matter of how we *do* act, but how we *ought* to act – we need to follow what is true. Then, once we have discovered the truth, we are to do our best to align ourselves to it. Our beliefs should be reflected in our behavior, but that isn't always the case. However, we should always do our best to ground our beliefs in solid reasoning anyway.

As I've proposed in this novel (particularly Chapter 20), we should carefully examine the truth claims of each religion and seek to determine which is true. It is my belief, based on my own research into the subject, that of all the religions in the world, Christianity best matches reality and can be defended logically and historically. Christianity is unique among the religions of the world, and it is my goal over the course of *The Tartarus Chronicles* to show how and why.

If you are not a Christian, I implore you to consider the claims of Christianity seriously. I would recommend books such as *The Case for Christ* by Lee Strobel, or *Evidence that Demands a Verdict* by Josh McDowell. Both authors were atheists who set out to disprove Christianity, only to have their beliefs changed after reviewing the overwhelming evidence confirming it. For other resources that I believe to be helpful, see the "Suggested

Resources" page at the back of this book. May God bless you as you seek the truth.

Seek and you will find.

Keith A. Robinson
October, 2012

Suggested Resources

Books

The Case for Christ by Lee Strobel
The Case for Faith by Lee Strobel
The Case for a Creator by Lee Strobel
Evidence That Demands a Verdict by Josh McDowell
World Religions in a Nutshell by Ray Comfort

Websites

www.apologeticsfiction.com - The official website for Keith A. Robinson.

www.apologetics315.com - A great hub listing other apologetics websites, podcasts and articles.

www.probe.org - The website for Probe ministries. Full of great articles and materials.

www.leestrobel.com - The official website for Lee Strobel. Also full of great videos, articles, etc.

www.answersingenesis - Although this website has mostly articles that deal with Creation/Evolution, there are many other great videos and articles available on a variety of topics regarding Christianity.

www.livingwaters.com - The website for Ray Comfort and Kirk Cameron's ministry.

About the Author

*K*eith Robinson has dedicated his life to teaching others how to defend the Christian faith. Since the release of *Logic's End*, his first novel, he has been a featured speaker at Christian music festivals and churches, as well as appearing as a guest on numerous radio shows. In addition, he is also the Extensions Director of the Creation Science Society of Milwaukee.

Since completing his *Origins Trilogy*, Mr. Robinson has been working on *The Tartarus Chronicles*, a new series of action/adventure novels dealing with the topic of world religions and worldviews.

When not writing or speaking, Mr. Robinson is a full-time public school orchestra director at Indian Trail High School & Academy, he serves as the Principal Violist of the Full Score Chamber Orchestra in Zion, Illinois, and he is a professional freelance violist and violinist in the Southeastern Wisconsin/ Northeastern Illinois area. He currently resides in Kenosha, Wisconsin, with his wife, Stephanie, their five children, an old-English sheepdog and a Rottweiler puppy.

CPSIA information can be obtained at www.ICGtesting.com
Printed in the USA
LVOW080712050613

336960LV00001B/102/P